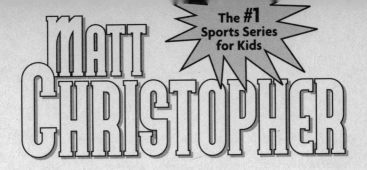

Matt Christopher

The #1 Sports Series for Kids

WINDMILL WINDUP

Text by Paul Mantell

Little, Brown and Company
Boston   New York   London

First Paperback Edition

Matt Christopher™ is a trademark of Catherine M. Christopher.

Library of Congress Cataloging-in-Publication Data

Mantell, Paul.
    Windmill windup : the #1 sports series for kids / Matt
Christopher; text written by Paul Mantell. — 1st ed.
        p.   cm.
    Summary: Thirteen-year-old Kelly, softball star, has to face new
challenges in her life, including assignment to a different softball
team and her mother's new boyfriend.
    ISBN 0-316-14531-9 (hc) / ISBN 0-316-14432-0 (pb)
    [1. Softball — Fiction.   2. Divorce — Fiction.   3. Mothers
and daughters — Fiction.   4. Family problems — Fiction.]
I. Christopher, Matt.   II. Title.
PZ7.M31835 Wi   2001
[Fic] — dc21   00-054599

10 9 8 7 6 5 4 3 2 1

COM-MO

Printed in the United States of America

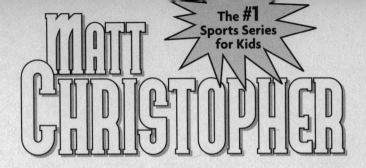

The #1 Sports Series for Kids

Matt Christopher

WINDMILL WINDUP

Text by Paul Mantell

Little, Brown and Company
Boston New York London

First Paperback Edition

Matt Christopher™ is a trademark of Catherine M. Christopher.

Library of Congress Cataloging-in-Publication Data

Mantell, Paul.
    Windmill windup : the #1 sports series for kids / Matt Christopher; text written by Paul Mantell. — 1st ed.
        p.   cm.
    Summary: Thirteen-year-old Kelly, softball star, has to face new challenges in her life, including assignment to a different softball team and her mother's new boyfriend.
    ISBN 0-316-14531-9 (hc) / ISBN 0-316-14432-0 (pb)
    [1. Softball — Fiction.   2. Divorce — Fiction.   3. Mothers and daughters — Fiction.   4. Family problems — Fiction.]
I. Christopher, Matt.   II. Title.
PZ7.M31835 Wi   2001
[Fic] — dc21   00-054599

10 9 8 7 6 5 4 3 2 1

COM-MO

Printed in the United States of America

1

Get two!" Kelly Conroy yelled. Tossing the softball up in the air, she swung the bat and sent a wicked ground ball toward third base. Karen Haynes grabbed it and whipped a sidearm bullet to second, where Sue Jeffers took the throw, pivoted, and threw on to Laurie Solomon at first to complete the double play. At least it *would* have been a double play, if this had been a real game.

It was only mid-March, but Kelly and her friends were already primed for spring softball season. "Awesome!" Kelly shouted approvingly. "And the Devil Rays get out of the inning!"

"Hit one out here, Kelly!" Nina Montone shouted from center field. "Gimme the patented Conroy Comet!"

"You asked for it!" Kelly shouted back, beaming. Swinging with all her might, she sent a rocket shot

1

Nina's way. The ball soared skyward, then kept going and going. Nina turned and started running, farther and farther, but the ball landed just beyond her reach.

"Are you kidding me?!" Karen said, laughing in amazement. "Man, have we got a cleanup hitter or what?"

"The Devil Rays are gonna be awesome this season," Sue agreed, pounding her glove and taking the relay throw from Nina. She tossed the ball softly back to Kelly, who stopped it with her bat.

"Hey, we weren't exactly chopped liver last fall," Kelly reminded them. "If Sue hadn't gotten the flu and missed the semifinals, we would've beaten the Giants and gone all the way."

"I don't care what you say," Laurie argued. "We're gonna be even better this time around. I mean, the Giants had half their squad move up to the next league, and we've got practically everybody back. We're gonna be unstoppable!"

"Yeah!" Sue shouted in agreement. "It's gonna be a Devil Ray dynasty!"

"Hey, you guys," Kelly said, tossing the ball softly up in the air. "Anybody up for pizza?"

A chorus of agreement came back at her, as the

half dozen girls who had gathered for this im-
promptu early practice trotted in toward home
plate. It was lunchtime, and Sammy's Pizza for
Sunday lunch had become a Devil Ray tradition.
Sammy's was where they had their weekly victory
celebrations — not only was it the best pizza in all of
Murphysville, but Sammy also made a mean ice-
cream soda, for anyone who could stomach pizza
and ice cream together.

"Man, we rule!" Kelly gushed as they gathered
their equipment and headed down Main Street
toward Sammy's. "I mean, think about it — who else
is gonna give us a run?"

"Nobody, that's who," Karen agreed. "We've got a
team full of all-stars, and the best coach on top of it."

"You said it! Coach Masur rocks!" Nina said. "Hey,
he said he's gonna teach us how to pitch windmill."

"Yeah, that's right — it's windmill pitching this
year," Kelly remembered. She wondered if she
could learn to do it. Up to now, she'd been the
team's first baseman — but being a pitcher sounded
pretty cool to her. Last year, she'd led the league in
home runs. With her big power swing, she could hit
the ball farther than any girl in the league.

She was fast on the base paths, too. Last season,

she'd stolen fifteen bases. Standing in line to order her two slices of Sicilian pizza with pepperoni, she imagined what it would be like to be the league's best pitcher as well — windmilling the ball so fast the hitters couldn't even see it.

She'd seen the U.S. women's softball team on TV, winning gold at the Olympics and the World Championships. One day, she wanted to be on that team — standing on the podium as the American flag was raised and "The Star-Spangled Banner" played. . . .

"Two Sicilian with pepperoni," Sammy the pizza man said, shoving a paper plate toward her. "Anything to drink with that?"

Kelly ordered a soda, paid, and brought her lunch to the big table the Devil Rays always shared. "Shove over," she told Sue Jeffers, giving her a push with her hip. Sue was her best friend on the team, except for maybe Karen Haynes.

But really, they were all friends, and over the last year and a half, they'd become almost a family. This coming fall, they'd all be moving up to the next league, scattered among a dozen different teams. But for now, they were still together — and this spring, they were going to win the championship.

Kelly munched thoughtfully on her pizza, letting the conversation wash over her like pleasant, hypnotizing white noise. Her thoughts drifted from this "family" to her own so-called family. Pathetic. Just her and her mom, ever since her dad had moved out two years ago.

Kelly loved her mom — a lot — but it wasn't much fun eating dinner just the two of them every night. Her dad had always been the happy-go-lucky one, keeping everybody laughing and gabbing. True, there was a lot of screaming between him and her mom after Kelly went to bed at night. But without him around, it was too quiet.

Kelly wished they would get back together someday and be a real family again. But she was pretty sure that would never happen. As her mom always said, her dad was "too irresponsible." Kelly knew it was true. Half the time, when he came to pick her up for his weekends with her, he was hours late. Every once in a while, he never even showed up. And though he always apologized sincerely, after the first few dozen times the apologies stopped meaning much.

No, she was much happier with her Devil Rays family than the one at home, Kelly thought. Here, she was accepted, looked up to, needed. She was right at the center of everything, practically the heart of the team. If the Devil Rays had had a captain, she was pretty sure she would have been it.

Today's practice had been her idea. Even though the team assignments hadn't come yet, Kelly knew the girls were all eager to get out there and play ball. She'd called Sue and Karen, and between them they'd managed to corral enough of the team to hold a practice without Coach Masur. They all knew he wouldn't mind. He'd be pleased they were working off the rust.

"Who's up for ice cream?" Nina asked, her mouth still full of pizza.

"Oh, not me." Kelly waved her off. "It's already three o'clock, and my mom'll be upset if I don't eat dinner."

"Come on, you're a growing girl!" Nina urged. "Look at you!"

Kelly blushed. At thirteen, she looked more like a grown woman than any of them. Even though she didn't wear any makeup, and despite the fact that jeans were her daily uniform, boys had begun to notice her. She'd had frequent invitations to the movies ever since last year, in sixth grade. Not that her friends were jealous, but they did love to tease her about it.

That was okay. Kelly could take it. She knew they all wished they had boys calling them up. As far as she knew, only Sue and Karen had had boyfriends. That was kind of why the three of them had become so close. They had that much more in common.

"Shut up!" Kelly told Nina, giggling. "You just want me to get fat."

"Hey," Nina pointed out, "the more you weigh, the farther you'll hit the ball."

That prompted a round of laughter and high-fives. Kelly got up, wiped her mouth with a paper napkin, gathered her trash, and headed for the door of the restaurant. "See you guys at school tomorrow," she said. With a wave, she pushed open the door and was out on the street again.

It was a beautiful Sunday afternoon, warm for this time of year. Kelly walked home slowly, enjoying the breeze and the scent of the first spring flowers in the air. Her house was only a few blocks away, just on the other side of the softball field. That was one of the best things about living where she did. When her dad had still lived with them, he'd taken her out every day after school to practice with her. That was why she'd gotten so good. He'd taught her everything she knew about softball, from the very first.

Kelly hadn't realized it at the time, but the reason her dad had been there for her every day after school was that he didn't have a steady job. Whenever he did get one, it never lasted. He always quit after a while, saying something or other was wrong with it — the boss, the pay, whatever. Her mom was always angry with him about it. It was one of the things they fought about the most.

Thinking back on it now, Kelly realized he probably liked taking her to the ball field to get away from thinking about his own problems. But it didn't matter to Kelly — for her, spending time with her dad like that had been heaven. Her fun, funny, affectionate, irresponsible dad. She missed him so much it made tears come to her eyes.

She wiped them away before turning her corner. The last thing she wanted was for her mom to see her upset and to have to explain why. Kelly and her mom were almost like sisters, now that it was just the two of them. They often spent evenings together watching TV, or playing cards, or just hanging out. Kelly loved her mom, but could tell she was lonely. Kelly couldn't blame her after fifteen years of mar-

riage. But then why had her mom insisted on getting a divorce?

Taking a deep breath, Kelly climbed the front steps and reached for the door handle. That's when she noticed the yellow note attached to the door. "Dinner in fridge. Have a nice evening. Love, Mom." Kelly pulled it off, sighing heavily. Notes like this usually meant only one thing — her mom had a date.

Dates for her mom didn't happen that often, and usually the guys didn't hang around very long, not once they found out that Mrs. Conroy had a daughter. Kelly's mom was pretty — redheaded like Kelly, but taller and slimmer, and with a bubbly, sweet personality. Kelly herself was much pricklier. When she had something on her mind, she just came right out and said it. Her mom usually found a way to make everything sound polite and nice.

Kelly pushed open the door. Once she stepped inside, she realized her mom hadn't actually left yet. Kelly could hear her singing softly to herself as she got ready upstairs. "Don't throw . . . bouquets at me. . . . People will say . . . we're in loooove."

Yuck. Kelly couldn't stand it when her mom got mushy like this. It usually meant she liked the guy

9

she was dating a lot and was only going to get her heart broken when he decided to drop the relationship.

"Hi, Mom!" Kelly shouted, loud enough so that her mom would hear her and stop singing.

"Hi, sweetie!" her mom's melodious voice came back. "Did you have a good practice?"

"The best," Kelly answered. "What's for dinner?"

"Meat loaf and mashed potatoes with creamed spinach, okay?"

"Do I get a choice?" Kelly asked sardonically.

"Nooo . . . ," trilled her mother.

"I didn't think so. Meat loaf will be fine. Where are you going?"

"To Il Capriccio."

"Fancy-shmantsy," Kelly said as her mom came tripping lightly down the stairs, almost dancing. She looked radiant and beautiful. Staring at her mother, Kelly hoped that when she was all grown up, she'd look as pretty.

"Of course you will," her mom always told her. "You are already." Kelly almost believed her, until her mom would add something like, "Besides, looks aren't all that count." That would make Kelly think her mom thought she was ugly — but only for a second. Kelly knew she was nice-looking. Why else

10

had Billy O'Donnell, the most popular boy in school, asked her to the spring dance last year?

"You're going out, huh?" Kelly said, a smile playing at one corner of her mouth. "Who's the new Romeo?"

"His name is Ken," her mother said, saying the name like it was sooo meaningful. *Kennnn.*

"Kennnn," Kelly repeated. "And that would make you Barbie?"

"That's right," her mom countered playfully. "I'm a living doll. Can't you tell?" Putting a finger to her cheek, Mrs. Conroy spun around like a doll. Kelly couldn't help laughing.

Then the doorbell rang, and her laughter froze in her throat. "Oh!" her mom gasped. "He's here already! Do I look all right?"

"You look fine," Kelly assured her. "You always look fine. Who cares, anyway?"

"What do you mean, who cares?" her mom said, frowning. She regarded Kelly suspiciously. "You be nice, now," she warned Kelly.

"Aren't I always?"

"No, you aren't, and you know it," her mom said, seriously worried now. "Don't blow this for me, Kel, okay? I like this guy."

Now it was Kelly's turn to frown. "Okay," she grumbled. "I'll be nice."

She hated Ken already. Who did this guy think he was, sweeping her mom off her feet like this?

Mrs. Conroy opened the door and said, "Hi!" in a breathy, nervous, too-loud voice. Ken smiled back. He was tall — well over six feet — and had long, dark hair and brown eyes. Kelly had to admit he was good-looking, but what she couldn't stand was the way he was staring at her mom.

"Hi, yourself!" he said back, giving Kelly's mom a big smile.

"Um, I'd like you to meet my daughter, Kelly," she said, stepping back so that Ken could come inside.

"Hi," Kelly muttered, holding her hand up in a lackluster wave.

"Hello, Kelly!" Ken said, beaming. He strode over to her, holding his hand out for her to shake. She held hers up limply and let him shake it, but she couldn't make herself look in his eyes.

Ken seemed a little taken aback by her cool reception. "Your mom has told me so many nice things about you," he offered.

"Uh-huh," Kelly said noncommittally.

Ken cleared his throat. "Well!" he said, clapping

his hands together and turning back to her mom. "Shall we go?"

"Yes, let's!" her mom said, keeping up the enthusiasm as best she could. "I'll just get my bag. . . ." She ran into the kitchen and came back a second later with her handbag. "Kelly, I'll be back by ten or so. You be good, okay, sweetie?" She gave Kelly a quick peck on the cheek, which Kelly did not return. "Bye now."

"Bye, Kelly! Nice meeting you!" Ken said with a wave. Slipping his arm through Mrs. Conroy's, he led her out the door and down the steps to his car, a boxy-looking sedan.

Kelly smirked. Her dad would never be caught dead in a car like that. He liked Corvettes and Mustangs and cool cars like that. Her mom always said he refused to grow up, but that was what Kelly liked best about him.

Her mom turned at the car door. "Oh, I almost forgot!" she called to Kelly. "There's a letter for you on the kitchen table!"

"Okay. Bye," Kelly said, closing the door and locking it. She sighed softly as the car drove off. She had the whole evening ahead of her, and nothing to do but watch TV or read. Alone.

She wandered slowly into the kitchen. Not that she was hungry — not after all that pizza — but she was curious about the letter. She rarely got mail, and she wondered if one of her friends had sent her a party invitation.

The letter was from the town's parks and recreation department. Oh, good. Her team assignment. Kelly tore the envelope open, just to see when the first Devil Rays' practice was.

She stopped breathing. She could hear her heart hammering inside her as she read the awful words. "KELLY CONROY: DIAMONDBACKS."

Oh, no! They'd put her on the wrong team!

2

The message of doom still clutched in her hand, Kelly ran for the door. She threw it open, yelling, "Mom! Wait!"

But it was too late. The car had already turned the corner and was accelerating onto Main Street. Kelly had a loud voice, but not *that* loud. Collapsing onto the concrete stoop, she put her head in her hands and moaned, "*Now* what am I going to do?"

She sat there for a long time — it seemed like hours to Kelly, but it was probably only five minutes or so — and finally, still utterly at a loss, she dragged herself to her feet and went back into the house.

How was it possible? Were they out to ruin her life, or what? Didn't they understand how important it was for a girl to stay with her teammates, especially when they were about to be champions? Not knowing what else to do, she went to the phone and dialed Sue Jeffers's number.

"Are you kidding me?" was Sue's stunned reaction. "You can't be on another team! We need you!"

"I know!" Kelly said, distraught. She waved the paper, which she still hadn't put down, as if Sue could see it. "But it says right here that I'm on the Diamondbacks."

"Omigosh — what if *everybody* got put onto a different team?" Sue gasped in horror. "I'll call you right back. I've gotta check." She hung up before Kelly could stop her.

"This is a nightmare," Kelly groaned, leaning her head against the refrigerator. Just for something to do, she pulled open the fridge and looked inside. The plate of meat loaf and mashed potatoes with creamed spinach stared at her. She usually liked her mom's cooking, but looking at the plate of food suddenly made her feel sick to her stomach. Just when she thought she was going to hurl, the phone rang and Kelly forgot all about her digestive troubles.

"Hello?"

"It's me," Sue said hurriedly. "Okay, I called Karen, Nina, Beth, and Laurie — they're all still on the team, and so am I. They're gonna check with everybody else, just to make sure."

"Great," Kelly said miserably. "So I'm the only one who's off the team?"

"It's got to be a mistake," Sue assured her. "Did you tell your mom?"

"I didn't get a chance," Kelly explained. "She's out with this new dorky guy she's seeing. Ugh."

"I know exactly what you mean," Sue commiserated. "My mom has the worst taste in guys. You'd think she'd let go of it by now. I mean, she's forty years old, for goodness' sake. But no, every once in a while she forgets and starts dating some new loser. It's always the same thing. The last guy was this airline pilot? Turned out he had a girlfriend in each of six different cities. Can you believe it?"

Kelly couldn't help laughing. Sue was such a hoot.

"Anyway, don't worry, they'll break up before you know it," Sue assured her. "Nobody wants to go out with a lady who's got a kid."

"You should have seen the phony smile he gave me," Kelly told her.

"I can just picture it," Sue said. "Anyhow, listen, about the team — it's some stupid mistake, I'm sure of it. I'll bet if you just call the commissioner and explain, he'll put you back on the team. Just tell him that —"

"Yeah, right," Kelly interrupted her. "Have you forgotten who the commissioner is?"

"Huh?"

"He's Lacey Jenkins's dad."

"Oh. Oops . . ."

Lacey, as Sue well knew, was Kelly's worst enemy.

"You've got to forgive and forget your feud with her," Sue advised sagely. "After all, it wasn't your fault that Billy O'Donnell liked you better than her."

"Yeah, tell that to Lacey," Kelly said, smirking.

"Besides, it's ancient history! That was back in sixth grade, for goodness' sake!"

Kelly sighed impatiently. "I can forgive all I want," she said. "But Lacey is not going to let her dad do me any favors. I'm telling you, Susie. It's a no-go."

"Well, you can at least try," Sue insisted. "What have you got to lose?"

"Okay, okay," Kelly said, giving in reluctantly. "I'll try talking with her tomorrow at school — even though she hasn't said a kind word to me in a year and a half."

"That's the girl," Sue said encouragingly. "You'll be surprised what a little friendliness can accomplish."

"You're right," Kelly shot back. "I *will* be surprised."

"Hey," Sue said, "you can catch more flies with honey than with vinegar."

"Hmm . . . where have I heard that before?" Kelly said, grinning in spite of herself.

She felt much better after she hung up with Sue, but soon the sense of dread returned. She found herself, as she often did in her weakest, lowest moments, punching in her dad's number on the memory dial.

The phone rang . . . and rang . . . and rang. Not that Kelly was surprised. Her dad was almost never home when she called him. And although she knew he had an answering machine — he was always leaving funny messages on it that cracked her up — as often as not, he forgot to turn the machine on.

She hung up, sighing deeply. It was no use. She was just going to have to live through the rest of this night with the great lump of worry in her stomach. Kelly felt worse than she had in years.

Oh well, she thought, shuffling into the living room and flipping on the TV, *maybe tomorrow will be better. At least it can't be worse.*

❁   ❁   ❁

But it *was* worse. Much worse. Kelly tracked down Lacey Jenkins in the cafeteria during lunch period. Lacey was at her usual table, with all the other popular, snobby kids Kelly hated. Fair was fair — they didn't like her much, either. Kelly wasn't surprised they held a low opinion of her after listening to Lacey trash her day after day. They sneered at her now as she approached with her heart in her throat.

"Um, hi, Lacey," Kelly said in a low voice.

Lacey looked at her, stunned, blinking rapidly. "Kelly Conroy?" she said, pronouncing the name like it was some deadly disease or some disgusting, slimy thing. "What are you doing here?"

"I, um . . ." Kelly felt her throat tightening. Suddenly, her knees were all rubbery, and she wanted to turn tail and run — or, at least, sink into the floor. "I just wanted to say hi," she mumbled lamely.

Lacey snorted. "Yeah, right," she said, sharing a skeptical laugh with her friends. "Just a friendly gesture, right?"

Kelly tried to smile, but her lips quivered, and she knew it must have looked more like a grimace, so she gave up.

"Just what is it you want?" Lacey challenged her. "That's the only reason you'd ever come over to me and say hi. So you might as well come out and ask me, so I can say no and get it over with."

"Um, no, you're wrong," Kelly lied. She was trapped, and she knew it — beaten before she'd even got started. "I just thought, let bygones be bygones, and like that. . . ."

"Well, aren't you little Mother Teresa?" Lacey quipped, sending her friends into sniggering fits. "Saint Kelly Conroy. Who do you think you are, anyway?" She turned her back to Kelly, and everyone at the table followed suit.

There was nothing for Kelly to do but back away and get out of there, so that's what she did. If she'd had a tail at that moment, it would have been between her legs as she skulked away.

Kelly kept walking until she was clear out of the cafeteria. She didn't want to talk to anybody while she was this shaky. She was afraid if she did, she'd burst into tears and embarrass herself. She made her way into the empty auditorium, where she sat down in the back row and composed herself, waiting for her next class, study hall.

Karen Haynes came in after a few minutes and saw her sitting there. "Kel!" she cried. Coming right over and sitting down next to Kelly, she gave her a

21

big, tight hug. Kelly, as she was afraid she would, burst into bitter sobs.

"Don't worry, kid," Karen assured her, rocking Kelly in her arms. "It's obviously just a simple mistake. A clerical error, like they say. I'm sure if you have your mom call the commissioner, he'll change you back. I mean, friendship is what softball league is supposed to be all about, right? Why would any grown-up want to break a kid's heart by separating her from her best friends? That would be so demented!"

Kelly wiped her eyes and gave Karen a broken, trembling smile before hugging her again, even tighter this time. Maybe Karen was right, she thought, daring to nurture some fragile hope. Lacey's father couldn't possibly be as mean as his daughter was. Maybe he didn't even know about the feud between her and Kelly.

Still, Kelly wasn't going to let her hopes get raised too high. In her experience, grown-ups didn't understand much about what kids wanted and why. You'd think they'd never been kids themselves.

3

Kelly got home from school before three-thirty, so she had to wait two whole hours before her mom got home. It was the slowest two hours in world history. She got all her homework done, although most of it was probably wrong, considering how hard it was to concentrate. The whole time, the TV blared music videos in the background. It distracted her, but it also kept her mind off her misery, so she made no move to turn it off.

By five o'clock, Kelly was going stir crazy. She knew her mom didn't like her to fill up on snacks right before dinner, but she couldn't help herself. She dove into the chips and salsa, and when they were gone, she made herself a plate of fruit, cheese, and crackers. At five-twenty, she started cleaning it all up so her mom wouldn't notice. Tonight, when Kelly said she wasn't hungry and didn't want any mashed potatoes or broccoli, she'd tell her mom it was because she was upset over the softball team. *Well, it's true, isn't it?* she thought.

Her mom didn't pull into the driveway until nearly six, and by that time Kelly was beside herself. "Hi, Mom!" she yelled, rushing out the door to give her a big hug.

"Well! Isn't this a nice greeting?" Her mom looked beautiful, Kelly noticed. Deep happiness seemed to well up out of her, beaming out of her sparkling blue eyes.

"I love you, Mom," Kelly said, trying not to show how upset she was.

"I love you, too, sweetie," her mom replied. Freeing herself from her daughter's grip, Mrs. Conroy went into the house and took off her trench coat. "Oh, I had such a fantastic day today!" she cooed. "Do you want to hear all about it?"

"Um . . . sure," Kelly said. She needed to ask her mom about calling the commissioner, but she figured it was better to wait for the right moment to ask for the favor.

"Well, I got to my desk, and there were two dozen long-stemmed roses on it, guess from who!"

"Uh . . . Ken?"

"Yes! Isn't that so romantic?"

Kelly suddenly felt the need to blow chunks. This was totally gross. Her mom was all gooey over this corny guy Ken, and all because he made goo-goo eyes at her and gave her flowers!

"Well, that was just the beginning," her mom went on, breezing into the kitchen and beginning to prepare food for dinner. "There were half a dozen e-mails from him on my computer. I did tell you he works in the office with me, right?"

"Uh, yeah. . . ."

"And the most amazing thing is that he's been there over a year, and we've barely looked at each other all that time. And now all of a sudden, wham! Isn't that amazing?"

"Amazing," Kelly repeated wanly. *Eeuw* — her mom was actually *in love!* She was acting like one of Kelly's middle school buddies. Kelly felt embarrassed for her.

"Well, then he came by my cubicle and whisked me off to lunch at this cute little bistro, and he told me — get this — he told me last night was the most wonderful time he'd had in years! Years! Oh, Kelly, I don't know when I've been this happy. Not since you were a very little girl, I can tell you. Oh, I hope you like him!" she said, suddenly worried.

Kelly tried to paste a smile on her face. "I guess he's okay," she said. What she wanted to say, but couldn't, was, "He's not as nice as Dad. How could you even look at another guy, when Dad's so fun, and handsome, and . . . and . . ."

But Kelly knew why her dad wasn't around anymore.

No wonder her mother liked Ken, with all the attention he was showering on her. Still, it was pathetic, Kelly thought. Who was this guy, anyway? Mom didn't even know him that well, and here she was, all gaga.

Kelly was so angry she could barely contain herself. She wanted to tell her mom to wake up and smell the coffee. She wasn't a girl anymore, so it was time to stop acting like one, for Pete's sake!

But she couldn't really say that. She didn't want to get on her mom's bad side — not tonight, at least. Not until her mom called the commissioner and got this awful mistake straightened out.

Kelly excused herself to go wash up for dinner. She needed to chill, no doubt about it. She went to

the bathroom and doused her face and hands with cold water, taking deep breaths and looking at herself in the mirror. She had the same strawberry-blonde hair and blue eyes as her mom, but with the frown on her face and the redness in her eyes from all the crying she'd been doing, she looked like the older of the two.

Kelly stayed there, working on looking neutral, until she was satisfied she didn't seem upset. Then she went down to dinner. She sat opposite her mom at the table as always, but just pushed her food around with her fork, not eating anything.

"What's the matter, honey?" her mom finally said, noticing for the first time that all might not be well with Kelly. "Is something bothering you?"

"I got put on the wrong softball team," Kelly told her.

"Oh, no!" her mom gasped. "You mean, you're not with Karen, or Sue?"

"Nope. None of them."

"But that's terrible! Oh, honey, I feel so bad for you. No wonder you aren't hungry!"

Looking down at her plate, Kelly pushed it slowly away from her.

"Oh, sweetie, I know how you must feel," her

mom said, reaching out and taking Kelly's hand. "Life is full of little disappointments like this —"

"Little disappointments?" Kelly repeated, aghast. She jerked her hand free. "Don't you understand? My life is over!"

"Now, now," her mom said reassuringly. "Don't be like that. You'll make new friends on your new team —"

"I don't want new friends!" Kelly shouted, bolting to her feet. "I don't want a new team! I want my old friends, on my old team!"

"Well, honey, sometimes we can't have things the way we want them —"

"Why not?" Kelly demanded, stamping her foot angrily. This was not coming out the way she'd intended it to, but it was too late now. "You could do something about it if you wanted to!" she insisted.

"What? What can I do, baby?" her mom asked.

"Call the commissioner and tell him you want me on the Devil Rays," Kelly said.

"I — well, I . . . I suppose I could call him, if it will make you happy. But I doubt —"

"Just call him, okay?" Kelly interrupted her. "I have to get back on my team! I have to!"

"All right," her mom sighed. "What's the number?" Pushing her chair back, she got up and went to the phone.

Kelly ran to her school student directory and looked up Lacey's number. She read it off to her mom, who punched it in. Kelly stood leaning against the kitchen island, not taking her eyes off her mom.

"Hello?" her mom said into the phone. "I'm the mother of a girl in your softball league. . . . Thirteen. . . . Yes, her name is Kelly Conroy."

There was a long pause while her mom listened, her brow furrowing. Kelly wondered if the commissioner knew who she was from Lacey. She even wondered if he'd taken her off the Devil Rays just to get back at her for his daughter's sake. It would have been the meanest move ever, but Kelly wouldn't have put it past Lacey to ask.

"Yes, well, it seems she's been put on a new team this season, and she's very unhappy. Yes, and so I was wondering if —"

There was another long pause. Then, "Yes. . . . I see. . . . Well, of course. . . . I understand. . . ."

Kelly was growing frantic. She gestured wildly to her mom, trying to get her to be more forceful. But being forceful wasn't in her mom's nature, and obviously she was being thoroughly intimidated by

Lacey's dad. Kelly could hear his loud, gruff voice coming through the phone speaker.

"Well, thank you, anyway. Yes. . . . Yes, I'll tell her." Her mom hung up the phone, then turned to Kelly with limpid eyes just brimming over with pity.

"Don't even say it!" Kelly screamed. "Don't talk to me! Don't talk to me ever again!" She grabbed a chair and shook it, then slammed it down on the floor.

"Kelly!" her mom said sharply. "Don't you even want to hear his reasons why?"

"What's the difference?" Kelly shot back. "He gave you a load of baloney, and you just stood there and took it! You didn't even try to convince him!"

"Of course I did!" her mom said weakly. "But the way he put it — he said they wanted more parity in the league — more equality between the teams, and that some of the teams, including yours, were too good, so they had to break them up to make things fairer. He said if he made an exception for you, he'd have to do it for everybody. So you see, it was hard to argue with him."

"Why? Why was it hard?" Kelly pressed her. "Aren't you my mother? Whose side are you on, anyway?"

"Yours, of course," her mom said.

"Yeah, right," Kelly said bitterly, turning away. "You're on nobody's side but your own." After throwing another chair to the floor, she ran up the stairs to her room and slammed the door behind her. Then she flung herself on her bed and wept bitterly, knowing that she'd never be a Devil Ray again.

The next day, Kelly sleepwalked through school. Math was a blur of numbers and symbols, and in science lab she nearly caused an explosion when she dropped her test tube and it shattered over the Bunsen burner. But the lowest point in her day came during gym, when she was approached by a girl she'd noticed around but never spoken to before.

The girl was pretty, with dark, shiny hair and dancing almond eyes. She was really good in gym, too. Kelly had noticed her doing the Project Adventure course. The girl seemed to have no fear of the rope apparatus and did the climbs faster than anyone else, pulling herself up and across the ceiling with powerful, athletic swings of her arms.

"Hi," the girl said. Kelly was sitting on the bleachers, trying to avoid being spotted by the gym teacher

31

and forced to do the rope course. "I'm Allison Warheit. Everyone calls me Allie."

"Allie, huh? I'm Kelly," Kelly said, shaking the girl's outstretched hand.

"You're in seventh grade, right?" Allie asked.

"Yeah. You?"

"Sixth."

That explained why Kelly had never run across her. "So how come you're in gym this period?" Kelly asked.

"I got advanced P.E.," Allie said.

Kelly frowned. She'd never even heard of advanced P.E., never mind been asked to be in it. How had this sixth-grader managed to get it? "Oh," she said, trying to act unimpressed.

"Hey, I heard you're on the Diamondbacks," Allie said, flashing a brilliant smile. "Me too!"

"Huh?" Kelly replied.

"You led the league in homers last year."

"Uh, yeah, I did," Kelly acknowledged.

"Cool. That's awesome that we're teammates, huh?" Allie said, clearly delighted.

"Yeah. Way cool," Kelly said unenthusiastically. Not that Allie noticed. She jogged away, waving over her shoulder to Kelly. "See ya!"

"Not if I see you first," Kelly muttered under her breath.

Great. It wasn't bad enough that she wasn't going to be on the mighty Devil Rays. Lacey Jenkins had gotten Kelly dumped onto a team full of sixth-graders!

They'd probably lose every game they played. She could see it now — Devil Rays 36, Diamondbacks 0. Football scores.

Why should she be in the softball league if it was no fun? After being so close to a championship, being on a loser team would be too painful to bear. Watching her friends hoist the trophy at season's end . . .

For the first time since she'd put on a mitt, Kelly Conroy began thinking about quitting altogether. Maybe just for this year. Maybe forever.

4

When she got home, Ken's car was in the driveway. Kelly could hear laughter coming from the kitchen. She opened and shut the door as loudly as she could, but she still caught them breaking away from each other. *Jeez,* Kelly thought with a shudder. They were probably *kissing!*

Her mom had a stirring spoon in her hand and was wearing an apron. Ken held the lid of a pot in his right hand and a fistful of spinach in his left. "Hi!" he greeted Kelly cheerfully. "We were just cooking up something yummy for dinner."

Kelly hated it when people said *yummy.* She didn't know why; she just did. "Oh, goodie," she responded in a lackluster voice. She crossed straight in front of him and threw open the fridge door.

"Honey, what are you looking for?" her mom

asked. "We're going to be eating in half an hour or so."

"I'm hungry now," Kelly said, rummaging in the fridge.

"Well, take some carrots and celery," her mom instructed her. "I don't want you to spoil your appetite."

"I don't feel like carrots and celery," Kelly said, grabbing a box of chocolate donuts, cold just the way she liked them. "I feel like a snack."

"Kelly," her mom said, her voice rising a bit. "You're not to eat that now."

Kelly ignored her, knowing that her mom usually gave up if Kelly paid no attention to her. She grabbed a donut from the box and was about to pop it into her mouth when she felt a strong hand grab her wrist tight.

"Your mother said you weren't to eat that now," Ken said sternly, pulling her hand away from her mouth. "Didn't you hear her?"

Kelly froze, anger rising in her like hot lava. She yanked her hand free of Ken's grip and spun around on him. "Who do you think you are?" she growled. "You're not my father. This is no business of yours!"

35

"Ken . . . ," her mom said, putting out a restraining hand.

"I'm sorry, Nora, but I can't stand to see you get disrespected like that," Ken said, shooting Kelly a reproving look.

"I don't even know you," Kelly said, staring daggers at him.

"Ken, she's had a tough week," her mom started to explain.

"You know, Nora, when I was a kid, my mother and father never let me talk to them like that, or ignore them. It sets a very poor precedent."

"Who cares what your parents did?" Kelly yelled. "Mom, tell him to stay out of this — it's not his business!"

"Ken . . . ," her mom began weakly.

"Nora, she's just manipulating you, and you're letting her."

"I know . . . you're right . . . it's just —"

"You know, you've got to set limits and lay down consequences." He turned to Kelly. "Do you know my son, Ryan? Ryan Randall?"

"Huh? Oh . . . yeah, I know who he is. He's an eighth-grader?"

"That's right. And you know, he hasn't given me

36

lip like that since he was a little boy. You know why? Because I wouldn't stand for it, that's why. I set strict limits for him, and it helped him mature. My kid knows not to treat his parents like that."

"Your kid doesn't even live with you anymore!" Kelly screeched. "That's how good a job you did!"

"Kelly!" her mom gasped, horrified. "You apologize right this instant!"

"I will not!" Kelly said. Spinning on her heels, she grabbed her donut off the countertop and ran up to her room before either of them could stop her. She slammed the door behind her and locked it, just in case they tried to barge in. She wasn't going to speak with her mother until Ken was out of the house. And as for Ken, she was never going to speak with him again!

She'd told him off, all right — but *good*. Who did he think he was, anyway? Next thing you knew, he'd be moving in with them and thinking he was her father and had a right to boss her around. Well, not if she could help it! Kelly decided then and there that she would do what she could to sabotage her mother's budding romance, for her mom's sake as well as her own.

She picked up the phone extension and punched

37

in her father's number. Lo and behold, he actually picked up the phone!

"Hello?"

"Daddy, it's me."

"Sugarplum! It's so great to hear your voice!"

"You too, Daddy."

"What's the matter, sugar? You sound upset."

"I am, kind of."

"Well, what is it? You know you can tell me."

"Well . . . I'm not so sure this time. . . ." Kelly let her voice trail off, just to make him curious.

"Hey, Kel. Didn't I always tell you you could count on me?"

"Well, yes. . . ." He'd told her, all right. But every time she'd done it, he'd let her down.

"Come on, tell me. There's nothing so terrible that we can't work it out together."

"Okay," Kelly said, figuring he was ready to hear it now. "There are two things, actually. First of all, they put me on the wrong softball team."

"What? The idiots!"

"I know. All my friends are on my old team, and it's an awesome team, too. So they decided to break up the team, and they put me on this team of sixth-grade losers!"

"Okay, okay, back up," her dad said. "Who made this decision?"

"The commissioner. And he's the father of this girl who hates me."

"Well, don't worry about a thing. I'll have a little talk with the guy, and then let's see what he says."

"Thanks, Daddy," Kelly said, a smile playing on her lips. "I asked Mommy to call him, but she didn't really try to convince him."

"Your mom's not exactly tough when it comes to things like this," her dad said in a forgiving, affectionate tone. Kelly could tell he still missed her, still loved her, even though she'd divorced him. "Okay, so that little problem's taken care of. What else is bothering you?"

Kelly cleared her throat. "Well," she said, "actually, it's about Mom. She's . . . well, she's got this new boyfriend. . . ."

There was a black silence on the other end of the line. "Oh?" her dad finally said, trying to sound casual and cover the obvious jealousy in his voice.

"Yeah. His name's Ken, and he's a total jerk. But Mom seems wild about him."

"Ken, huh?" Her dad's voice was thick with anger and frustration.

"He tries to act like he's my father or something," Kelly told him. "But I let him know he wasn't."

"Good girl," her dad told her. "Well, don't worry. Your mom's not stupid. If this guy's half the jerk you say he is, she'll figure it out soon enough."

"I don't know," Kelly said tauntingly. "She seems pretty gaga, if you ask me. . . ."

"She does, huh? Well, I'll have a little talk with her, too."

"Thanks, Daddy. I knew I could count on you." Kelly hung up, feeling very naughty, but not sorry. She knew she'd tossed a bomb. Now it was just a matter of waiting for it to go off.

5

Kelly was feeling more upbeat the next morning when Sue Jeffers and Karen Haynes caught up to her at her locker before school. "Well?" Sue asked, breathless. "Any progress?"

"Mmm . . . not yet," Kelly said, smiling mysteriously.

"You know, today's our first practice. We start playing games next week," Karen said.

"Are you gonna get switched or aren't you?" Sue asked. "Because if you aren't, Beth Parks wants to play first base."

"Beth? She's an outfielder," Kelly moaned. "She's not used to taking ground balls."

"Oh, and Laurie is gonna pitch," Karen said. "She went to this clinic over the winter and learned how to pitch windmill."

Kelly felt a sharp pain in her side, a pang of loss

41

and regret. "Don't worry," she said, a little too confidently. "My dad is going to tell off Mr. Jenkins."

"Seriously?" Karen asked, her eyes growing wide.

"Is he gonna threaten to beat him up?" Sue wondered.

"Probably." Kelly shrugged. "I don't know. He told me not to worry about it, that he'd take care of it."

Kelly noticed a quick exchange of doubtful glances between Sue and Karen. She knew they were remembering all the times Kelly'd said her dad was coming to see them play, only to have him not show up.

But this time was going to be different, Kelly told herself. She was sure her dad had heard the pain in her voice. He knew how important this was to her. This time, he wouldn't let her down.

"Maybe I'll cut out of my team's practice and come over to work out with you guys," Kelly suddenly said.

"Cool!" Sue said.

"Awesome!" Karen added.

"I mean, I'm going to be back with the Devil Rays after tomorrow, so why not, right?"

"Um, right!" both girls said in hesitant unison.

"Cool," Kelly said, nodding with finality. "See you

guys then." Closing her locker, she headed down the hall toward her first class.

Murphysville Park had four softball fields, placed in the four corners of the park so that their outfields merged into one if you went back far enough. This made for a lot of home runs, since hard-hit balls kept rolling and rolling till they wound up in the infield of another diamond, in the middle of somebody else's game!

In the week before the opening of softball season, four teams could practice at once from 3:00 to 5:00 P.M. From 5:00 to 6:00, teams played each other in pickup games, to give the players the feeling of real game action. Since there were now ten teams in the league, this meant that each team could practice only every third day. So every practice was important, and Kelly meant to get the most out of every minute.

That was why, instead of heading over to field number three, where the Diamondbacks were gathering, she strode right over to field number one, where her beloved Devil Rays were already taking serious fielding practice.

Kelly had stuffed her old Devil Rays jersey into

her backpack that morning. Now she slipped it on, changed into her spikes, flexed her mitt, and stuck her hand into it, ready to begin another great season. "Yo, guys!" she called out, trotting over to exchange hugs and high-fives with her homegirls.

"Conroy!" Coach Masur cried happily, waving the bat at her. "What happened with you?" He put down the bat and walked over to first base, where Kelly was now surrounded by her teammates. "I fought and fought to get you, but the commissioner said no way. You in trouble with him or something?"

"His daughter hates me," Kelly said, not caring who heard her say it. "He did it just for spite. Isn't that demented?"

"Well, now, wait a minute," Coach Masur said, putting a hand on her shoulder. "I'm sure that's not why. You know, they did add two new teams, and we all lost good players in the draft. I was just kiddin' about you being in trouble with him."

"It's okay," Kelly told him. "My dad's going to get me back on the team."

"Is that a fact?" Coach said, raising his eyebrows in surprise. "Well, let's hope so, huh?"

"Yeah. So I thought I'd practice with you guys today."

"Ahem . . . well, that wouldn't be a good idea," Coach Masur said, clearing his throat and staring at the ground.

Kelly shrank back, stunned. "W-why not?" she asked.

"Well, your other coach will be counting on you to be there, Kelly," Coach Masur explained. "That team needs you."

"And you guys don't? Is that what you're saying?"

"You know that's not what I mean," Coach Masur said. "We've got the cleanup spot reserved for you, along with first base — *if* you get switched back to us. But until then, I've only got three practices to prepare my team for the first game. I've gotta find a new first baseman, see who can pitch windmill, and who's new that can try to fill your very big shoes."

Kelly sniffed back the tears that she felt coming. "Are you saying I've got big feet?" she tried to joke. She burst out laughing and crying at the same time.

Coach Masur gave her a tight hug. "Hey, Kelly, believe me, if I could have changed it, I would have. I hope your dad has better luck than I did. And if he doesn't, you're gonna have a great season anyway. It just won't be for us and nobody's sorrier about that than I am."

"Thanks, Coach," Kelly said in a voice no louder than a whisper. "Bye, guys. See you at the next practice, after I get switched." Wiping her nose with her sleeve, she picked up her stuff and walked slowly into the outfield, headed for field number three.

"Kelly!" A girl came running toward her from first base. It was Allie Warheit, the one who'd tried to make friends with her in school the other day.

Why is she being so nice? Kelly wondered. *She doesn't even know me!*

Kelly didn't want to make friends with Allie, or with any of these kids. What for, anyway? Tomorrow, she wouldn't even be with this team anymore — *probably. . . .*

"Hi!" Allie greeted her, flashing such an irresistible smile that Kelly couldn't help smiling back. This girl was just so thrilled to see her, it was almost weird.

"Do you want first base?" Allie asked her. "I've always played first, but I know you did, too, and so if you want it, it's okay. I could play short or something. Or maybe even pitch."

"Yeah," Kelly said, trying to make herself sound tough. "First." She really was touched, though. "That's nice of you, Allie."

"Oh, that's okay," the other girl said, flashing that smile again that was just like a light bulb lighting up.

"'Kay," Kelly said. She dumped her gear on the bench, then went to meet the coach, a tall, gawky-looking guy with glasses, who was wearing a T-shirt, khaki shorts, big sneakers with no socks, and a yellow Diamondbacks hat. He looked like some big wading bird — or like a kid who was lousy at sports, but was now all grown up.

"Hi, I'm Kelly Conroy," she said, holding up a hand in greeting.

"Hey! Nice to see ya!" the man said, shaking hands. "I'm Coach Beigelman. Welcome to the team!"

Ugh. Kelly nodded, but couldn't manage a smile. She couldn't even look the guy in the eye.

"Okay, Diamondbacks!" Coach Beigelman called out. "I think we've got a quorum, so let's start our practice. First of all, I think we should introduce ourselves to each other. So please share your first and last names, what grade you're in, and what position you want to play."

Kelly listened as the girls took turns introducing themselves. She knew some of the players, of course. It was a collection of girls from other teams,

47

plus a few girls whose parents had filled out the applications after the deadline and so got shunted onto the last team available.

Five of the Diamondbacks were sixth-graders, including Allie Warheit. Of the seventh-graders, a few were good athletes, but one or two were just hopeless. This was not going to be pretty.

"Oh, boy," Kelly said under her breath, "I get to be the star of the worst team in softball history."

"Okay." Coach Beigelman applauded them when they were done with the introductions. "I want you to know that we're all here to have fun first of all and that no matter what happens out on the field, to me, you're all winners!"

Oh, brother, Kelly moaned inwardly. He was going to be big on the rah-rah, and nonexistent on the fundamentals. A perfect coach for a team full of losers!

"Okay, everybody out to the positions you asked for!" the coach yelled. "Go, D'backs!"

The girls cheered, except for Kelly. They all made their way into the field at various speeds. Some, eager to claim a favorite position, ran to be the first one there. Others, who cared less or just reacted slower, jogged or walked into position, taking their places behind the early birds.

Kelly ambled slowly out toward first base, where Allie and four other girls were standing. They all backed away and let Kelly position herself at the bag. Everyone knew who Kelly Conroy was. Everybody, it seemed, but Coach Beigelman.

"Okay, let's get one!" he shouted, then tossed the ball up and tried to hit a grounder. He missed, and the ball dropped to the ground.

"Brother," Kelly muttered, shaking her head.

"Okay, okay, here goes." Again he missed, and then a third time. "Um, would any of you like to hit grounders to the team?"

"I'll do it," Kelly said, a smug smile playing across her face. Let Allie play first. She, Kelly, would hit these kids some real grounders. She would see soon enough how good they really were.

Kelly shot a vicious ground ball at the third baseman. The girl let the ball scoot right between her legs into the outfield.

"Nice try!" Coach Beigelman said gently. "You'll catch the next one!"

Not unless you tell her to keep her glove down,

Kelly thought disgustedly. It was a good thing she wasn't going to be on this team for long.

The shortstop ducked when Kelly sent a hard line drive her way. "Stay with it! Stay with it!" Coach Beigelman said, clapping his hands together for encouragement.

The second baseman managed to knock the ball down when Kelly hit it to her. Picking it up, the girl then threw high and wide to first. Allie Warheit stretched, briefly left the ground, then came down in a split, with her right toe still touching the bag.

"Great play, first base!" Coach yelled excitedly. "Hey, we've got an all-star!"

An all-star, huh? Kelly thought, suddenly angry at Allie. *Okay, all-star, try this one on for size!* Kelly sent a wicked line drive to Allie's right, far off the bag. Allie leaped, reached out, and snagged it. The ball nearly ripped the glove out of her hand, but she held on for a miraculous catch.

"Wow!" Coach Beigelman crowed. "I think we've found our first baseman, huh? Okay, girls, let the next one behind you have a turn."

Kelly was steaming mad. *Just like that, a stupid sixth-grader makes a couple of lucky plays and takes my position away?* she thought indignantly. Who did Allie Warheit think she was? Boy, she was sneaky, too — the way she'd offered Kelly the position, acting like she didn't want it. . . .

The fact that Allie had had nothing to do with Kelly's decision to abandon the position and hit grounders never occurred to her. It only counted that, for the moment at least, Allie had stolen the first baseman's job away from her.

Not that she even *wanted* to be the Diamondbacks' first baseman. She didn't even want to *be* on this team!

"Coach?" Allie suddenly called out.

"Yeah?"

"Could I try out for shortstop instead?"

"Are you kidding? Stay right where you are!"

"Um, it's just that, well, Kelly's so great at first base. . . ."

"Kelly?"

"Me, Coach," Kelly said, reminding him who she was.

"Oh! Right. Well, okay, go on out there, and Allie, you take short."

The poor girl who'd ducked took her place behind

Allie. No one else had even tried out for short. Apparently, none of these girls felt confident enough to handle the position, one of the toughest on the field.

"Okay," the coach said. "I'll try again here with the hitting. I'm a little rusty. Kyla," he called to the first shortstop, "come on in here and play catcher for me. Catch it when the first baseman throws the ball in."

The scared girl trotted awkwardly in and proceeded to take on her new assignment. The coach began hitting grounders, and it was soon apparent that Allie Warheit could play any position she wanted to.

Even Kelly was impressed. She had nothing against this girl, now that she'd stopped trying to compete with Kelly. And for a sixth-grader, she was awesome in the field. If she could hit at all . . .

She could. When they took their turns hitting batting-practice pitches from the coach, Allie nearly took his head off with her first line drive. She sprayed balls all over the outfield — every one of them a lined shot. No pop-ups, no grounders. With her compact, level swing, she never missed a pitch that was anywhere near the zone.

Kelly stepped up for her turn, determined not to

be upstaged. When the coach threw her his first pitch, she sent it screaming skyward. The ball traveled so far that someone in the outfield of field number four turned around and caught it on the fly!

"Wow!" Coach Beigelman gasped. "Have we got a cleanup hitter, or what?"

Kelly couldn't help smiling a grin of secret satisfaction. She hit the next three pitches even farther.

"Okay, enough hitting!" Coach Beigelman said, throwing his hands up. "I'm getting embarrassed here. Let's see how you girls run the bases."

It turned out that Allie Warheit was fast, too — even faster than Kelly, who'd been the fastest girl on the Devil Rays. For a minute, Kelly started to fantasize about herself and Allie leading the Diamondbacks into battle . . . but then she caught herself. There was no way this team could win with just the two of them. And as nice as Allie was, Kelly could never see herself making friends with her off the field. She was a sixth-grader, after all. It would just be too embarrassing. Totally uncool.

Besides, she wasn't going to be here long. Once her dad talked with the commissioner, she'd be back with her old buddies again in no time.

6

Kelly could hear the shouting before she even turned the corner onto her street. She knew instantly what was happening. It sounded exactly the same as all those other times, in the last two years before her mom and dad's marriage had broken up.

As she neared the house, the sounds grew clearer, and she could make out some of the words. "What kind of parent —?" "— Your business to spy on my social life?" "Keep an eye on my daughter!" Kelly could see his car, a gold Firebird from the '70s with two new dents in it, parked in the driveway.

Kelly was going to wait until the fight was over and her dad had left before going inside. She didn't want to get into the middle of everything. But just then it began to rain, and Kelly could hear thunder getting closer. She opened the kitchen door and went into the house.

There they were, in the living room. It was a scene out of nightmares past. Her dad was pacing the living room, tossing magazines on the floor and kicking them around as he raved on and on about her mom and Ken.

"You've really lost it this time," her mom was saying, shouting to get through to him. "Ken's brother is a lawyer, you know. If you ever threaten him again —"

"*That* sounds like a threat to me," her dad countered, waving an accusing finger.

"And if you call me at my office again," her mom went on, oblivious to his taunts, "I'm going to have to take legal action."

"Take it!" her dad yelled. "I'm going to take some action myself. What kind of a mother do you think you are, running around and leaving my little girl home alone?"

"It was just for the evening," her mom tried to explain. "She's almost fourteen, Bill."

"A baby!" her dad insisted. "And she was put on the wrong team because of your neglect!"

"My *neglect?* Bill, we are not married anymore. Do you get it? It's over! It's been two years! Have you read the divorce papers lately? Or the custody agreement?"

"We'll see about custody!" he snapped back. He reached for the door and yanked it open. "You'll be hearing from *my* lawyer!" As he was about to step through the doorway, he caught sight of Kelly for the first time. "Oh — hi, angel," he said, trying unsuccessfully to smile. "Your mother and I, um . . ."

"Your father is just leaving, Kelly," her mom needlessly informed her. "If you have anything to say to her, Bill, make it quick. You're trespassing."

"I'll . . . I'll call you, baby," her dad said, blowing her a kiss and starting to close the door.

"Wait! What about the team?" she asked, then held her breath.

"The team?" her dad repeated dumbly. "Oh! Yeah . . . look, I spoke to the guy, and, um . . . I'm not through trying, angel —"

"He said no, didn't he?" Kelly said softly.

"Well, he didn't exactly use that word. . . ."

"What happened, Bill? Did you threaten him, like you threatened Ken?" her mom blurted out. "You did, didn't you! I'll bet you got him so ticked off that he hung up on you!"

Her dad turned to her mom, his eyes blazing. "I hear *your* method of persuasion produced a big fat zero results!" he shot back.

"You have got to get ahold of your temper, Bill."

"Don't tell me what to do!" He was about to go on, but then thought better of it and turned again to Kelly. "Sorry, baby. Like I said, I'll keep trying. . . ."

"Sure," Kelly said, her voice a mere whisper. "Bye, Dad."

"Bye, sugar." He shut the door softly. A minute later there was the sound of burning rubber, and he was gone, speeding down the wet street, his taillights disappearing into the distance.

"I'm sorry you had to walk in on that," her mom said, coming over to hug Kelly.

Kelly shrugged her off. She wasn't feeling good now, toward either of her parents. Her dad was acting like a jerk, sure. But her mom hadn't exactly stuck up for her with the commissioner, either. And besides, her mom was making a total fool of herself with Ken. Her dad was right about that much.

"I'm sorry, Kelly," her mom repeated. "How was practice today?"

It was the absolute wrong question. Kelly burst into bitter sobs. When her mom tried to comfort her, Kelly wrenched herself from her grasp, yanked open the door, and went running out into the stormy night.

"My life is one big misery!" Kelly moaned to Sue, while her friend used a pair of big bath towels to dry her off from the soaking she'd undergone on her way over there. Kelly held her hands out to her sides so Sue could dry them. "My mom is seeing Mr. Cornball Ken, my dad is acting like an idiot, just like he used to do — no wonder my mom left him — and nobody cares if I live or die!"

"Oh, come on, Kel," Sue said with a smile, fishing out a set of dry clothes for Kelly to put on. "You're exaggerating. Look, I know how you feel. My parents are divorced, too, remember. And life around here is no picnic. My mom dates some of the biggest losers around. And my dad lives in Anchorage, Alaska. I'm lucky if I see him once a year. So, okay, I'm on the Devil Rays and you're not, but —"

A moan from Kelly stopped her. "Sorry," Sue said

quickly. "Didn't mean to touch a raw nerve. It's rotten luck, I know. That stupid Lacey. She is such a nit."

"She hates me," Kelly said, letting Sue throw a sweatshirt over her head. "And my team is a bunch of losers, too. You should see them."

"I'll be seeing them soon enough. We play you guys in the first game of the season."

Kelly spun around, wild-eyed. "What!"

"Didn't you look at your schedule?" Sue asked, blinking. "Yeah, first game's in three days. You'd better hurry if you want to get switched."

"Forget it. There's no chance," Kelly told her. "My dad blew up at the commissioner."

"Oh, god," Sue said, sinking down on the edge of the bed next to Kelly. "Boy, no wonder you're depressed."

"You see?"

"I do. But Kel?"

"Yeah?"

"Don't go jumping off a bridge when we beat you, okay? I mean, we can't go soft on you guys or anything. We have to win the championship, y'know?"

"Sure," Kelly said, feeling lower than a worm. "Go ahead. Stomp all over our pathetic bones."

"Aw, Kelly. Isn't there anyone on your team who you like?"

"No," Kelly groaned. "Well, just this one girl, Allie. She's a sixth-grader, though. She's so pathetic, the way she keeps trying to make friends with me."

"What's pathetic about that?" Sue wanted to know.

"Duh, are you thick?" Kelly asked sarcastically.

"Kelly, who cares what anybody thinks? It's okay to be friends with a sixth-grader."

Kelly gave her a long, hard, searching look.

"Well, okay, I personally would not do it, but it's better than having nobody on your team you like."

Kelly sighed. She wondered if Sue really meant what she was saying, or if, by tomorrow, everyone at school would be whispering about how desperate Kelly Conroy had gotten.

When she got home, there was another car in the driveway — Ken's. Obviously, her mom had wasted no time, calling him the moment she'd run out the door and crying to him to come over and comfort her in her misery. Yuck. Kelly went inside, shaking her head in disgust.

She stopped short when she came into the dark living room. Someone was sitting there in the shadows! Kelly let out a little gasp and froze when an unfamiliar male voice said, "Hello."

Kelly inched backward and reached out to turn on the lights. A boy was sitting on the couch, his arm up in front of his face to shield his eyes from the sudden glare.

He looked about fifteen, with long, straight, shiny, dark hair and a tall, slim frame. He lowered his hand and she saw that his face, with its long lashes covering his large brown eyes and its strong jaw, was familiar to her. He looked like Ken.

"It's me, Ryan Randall," he said. "We met once in French, before I got transferred to the AP class. Remember?"

"Um, yeah!" Kelly said, a little too quickly. She sort of remembered, but not really. "I know I've seen you around a few times."

"Yeah. Eighth-graders and seventh-graders don't mix much, I guess," he said, giving her a small smile.

Kelly couldn't help noticing how cute he was, even if he was kind of shy. She knew from the grapevine that he was really smart and sometimes hung out with the kids in the computer club. But she also knew that Ryan was supposedly one of the stars of the middle school's baseball team.

"Where's my mom?" Kelly asked.

Ryan motioned with his head toward the stairs. "Up there," he said. "With my dad."

"Oh." There was an uncomfortable silence.

Ryan broke it. "Your mom's nice," he said, giving Kelly a little smile.

"Yeah, she is. Sometimes," Kelly agreed halfheartedly. She did not say that Ken was nice, too.

"My dad's a good guy, once you get to know him," Ryan assured her, picking up on her train of thought.

"Really?" It was half a question, half a sarcastic remark.

"I guess you and he haven't been getting along, huh?"

"Do *you* get along with him?"

"He's my dad," Ryan reminded her with a shrug. "He's kind of strict," he elaborated when she didn't answer. "But he's always there for me, even though he doesn't live with us anymore. He comes to all my ball games and stuff."

"You're on the team, right?"

"Yeah, I pitch for them."

"Really?"

"Uh-huh."

Kelly went to the foot of the stairs and listened. She could hear her mom crying softly, and Ken's kind voice comforting her. With a sigh, she sat down across from Ryan.

"My dad is pretty nuts about your mom," he told her.

"She likes him a lot, too," Kelly said, sighing again.

"Maybe they'll be good for each other," Ryan suggested hopefully.

"Don't you want your mom and dad to get back together?" Kelly asked.

Ryan shrugged. "They were pretty miserable, if you ask me. He seems much happier now, and she's not doing so badly, either. She's got a new career and stuff."

"Oh." Another uncomfortable silence fell. Now that they were done talking about their parents, there seemed to be nothing to say. Kelly couldn't look at him, except when he wasn't looking at her. And he seemed to look away every time she raised her eyes to his. It was beginning to feel weird.

Kelly knew that the reason she was uncomfortable was that she thought Ryan was cute. But she assumed his discomfort was because . . . well, because here he was, having to sit around with some dorky, shy seventh-grader.

"So . . . you play ball, huh?" she said, and immediately felt stupid.

"Yeah . . . you?" he asked, obviously not wanting to talk about himself.

"Uh . . . yeah . . . softball, actually," Kelly said. Why, oh why, was everything out of her mouth sounding so dumb?

"Oh. Wow," Ryan said, nodding slowly.

This was torture. Kelly couldn't stand it anymore. Luckily, at that moment the grown-ups came back downstairs, and pretty soon, after a few quick pleasantries, Ken drove off with Ryan.

"So," her mom said when they were alone again. "Where did you go off to?"

"To Sue's," Kelly said dully.

"Did you and Ryan get acquainted?"

"Mom!" Kelly said in an annoyed tone. "What are you, the Spanish Inquisition? Stop asking me so many questions!" She stormed upstairs — and all the way to her room, she could feel her mom's inquiring eyes following her.

7

The Diamondbacks' next practice was almost as bad as the first, but not quite. Some of the sixth-graders on the team were actually good — Allie most of all, of course. Kelly thought that a year from now the Diamondbacks might actually have a team. Of course, she'd be on to the next league by then, so it wouldn't benefit her any.

Coach Beigelman spent most of his time trying to find someone who could pitch windmill. Nobody actually knew how, including him, so it was difficult. For most of batting practice, it was just Marie del Toro, a total klutz, soft-tossing to the hitters.

Kelly, Allie, and even some of the girls who weren't very good were smacking the ball all over the place. "Hey, we've got a hitting powerhouse here!" Coach Beigelman exclaimed enthusiastically.

But Kelly knew that once they started facing real pitching the Diamondbacks' bats were going to go cold in a hurry.

When the day of their first game arrived, Kelly could not keep down her sense of dread. This was all so unreal! As she waved to all her friends on the other team, it felt like the old days in T-ball, when one team was short of players and the other team would lend them some for the day. Except in those cases, you would always give the other team your worst players. Kelly was one of the Devil Rays' best, or rather, ex-best.

She went over to greet her pals. They all seemed happy enough to see her, but Kelly could tell they were concentrating on getting ready for the game. The Rays were such a together team, they weren't about to let themselves get distracted over a reunion with Kelly.

"Good luck today," Sue was kind enough to say to her. "You guys are gonna need it. No offense."

Kelly shrugged and sighed sadly. "I can't believe this is happening," she said. "It's such a nightmare."

She swallowed hard so she wouldn't start crying. She gave Sue a quick hug before running back to the other bench, where the Diamondbacks were all staring at her like she was a traitor or something for talking with the enemy.

"They're friends of mine, okay?" Kelly said to their accusing faces.

"Okay, okay, team!" Coach Beigelman said, clapping his hands to get their attention. "I want you all to play hard today and do your best, and may the best team win. But remember, it's how you play the game that counts!"

"Oh, brother," Kelly said under her breath. "Spare us, please."

Coach Beigelman gave out the starting lineup. Kelly was batting cleanup, of course, with Allie just ahead of her in the third spot. Dorien Day, a skinny little sixth-grader who could run really fast, was leading off. Kyla Sutton was second, with Rena Downey fifth. The bottom of the order was composed of three sixth-graders and poor, hopeless Marie del Toro, batting ninth.

"We're the visiting team, so we're up first," the coach said. "Let's jump out to a lead, okay? That'll give Marie a cushion to work with."

"She's gonna need it," Kelly muttered softly.

"What's that?" Dorien asked her.

"Um, nothing," Kelly said.

"Okay. Here goes . . ." Dorien picked up a bat that was much too heavy for her, in Kelly's opinion, and headed for home plate.

"Play ball!" the umpire shouted, and put on his mask.

Laurie Solomon was on the mound for the Devil Rays. Kelly watched her warm up. Wow! Where had she learned to windmill pitch like that?

Kelly had never known Laurie to have such a great arm. Obviously, she'd been getting good coaching somewhere. The ball zipped in toward the plate like a blur, making a sharp, buzzing sound. Kelly felt her muscles tightening and her nerves jangling. She'd never had to hit fast pitching like that before. Would she be able to now?

"Okay, here we go, Diamondbacks!" Coach Beigelman said in his typical enthusiastic tone. "Put your hands in here!" The sixth-graders really got into the spirit, but Kelly and some of the other older girls laid back when he tried to get them excited. It seemed so . . . well, *dumb*.

Kelly took a seat on the bench as the ump called, "Play ball!" and the Diamondbacks came up to bat.

Dorien went down on strikes, swinging wildly at pitches she couldn't even see, half of which were over her head. Kelly snorted to herself and shook her head. This new team of hers was hopeless. How she wished she was back on her old team, where she belonged!

Kyla Sutton was next. She had two strikes on her before a wild pitch from Laurie nailed her right in the helmet. Kyla screamed, more in fright than in pain, as Coach Beigelman and the ump checked to see if she was all right. She got up, wiped the tears from her eyes, and was escorted to first base.

Kelly blew out a long breath. That was a close one, she realized. Kyla had been lucky not to get hurt. Laurie was pitching fireballs, and she was just a little bit wild, too. A scary combination.

Now, as Kelly grabbed a helmet and a bat and stood in the on-deck circle, Allie Warheit stepped up to the plate. Allie watched the first three pitches go by without swinging, letting the count go to two balls and a strike. A hitter's count. Then she swung at the fourth pitch and sent the ball rocketing over the center fielder's head.

Allie took off like a shot, and by the time she rounded third base, she had caught up to Kyla, who was still recovering from being hit in the head by the pitch.

"Go! Go!" Allie shouted, pushing Kyla along in front of her. The two girls crossed the plate ahead of the relay throw, and the Diamondbacks mobbed them, yelling happily as they took a 2–0 lead.

Kelly walked slowly to the plate, a mix of emotions surging inside her. She'd hoped to be the one to knock the runner in, but Allie Warheit had stolen her thunder. Now there was no way Kelly could top her feat. Not in this at bat, anyway.

Laurie Solomon wound up and fired a pitch. Kelly tried to get the bat moving through the zone, but the ball was in the catcher's mitt before she even swung. "Strike one!" the umpire called. Kelly tensed, gripping the bat handle tighter. She knew she'd have to hurry her swing to catch up with the ball.

Laurie fired another one, and Kelly swung fast — but the pitch was outside and high, and she wound up lunging at it, hitting only air. "Strike two!" the umpire called.

Kelly could hear the murmuring from both benches. Everyone knew her reputation from last season — the big home-run hitter, best in the league. But that had been against regular, slow pitching, not windmill. Kelly tensed even harder, determined not to let the next pitch get by her.

Laurie went into her windup and let fly. Kelly could see that the pitch was in the dirt, but she'd had to start her swing so early that now she couldn't stop it in time. On a check swing, the umpire yelled, "Stee-rike three! Yer out!"

Kelly slammed her bat on the ground and headed back to the bench, blinking back sudden tears. She glared at everyone who told her, "That's okay, Kelly," or "Next time, Kel." She didn't want to hear it. She'd been humiliated. That stupid Allie Warheit had hit a home run like it was nothing, and she, the great Kelly Conroy, had whiffed like a total loser.

In the bottom of the first, things started to get really bad. Still thinking about her strikeout, Kelly got a late jump on a grounder, and it got through her for a base hit. It could even have been considered an error.

Her miscue opened the door for a seven-run Devil Ray avalanche against the lame pitching of Marie del Toro, the Diamondbacks' starter. By the end of the inning, Marie had been replaced by Dorothy Barad, one of the sixth-graders, and the D'backs were in a hole that would only get deeper as the game went on.

Kelly batted again in the third inning and once

more in the fifth. Each time she whiffed badly, and the murmuring on both benches got louder. Now, when she tromped back to the bench, the other girls avoided her, seeing what an evil mood she was in. No one wanted to get her head bitten off by trying to console her.

Kelly could feel the stares of her former teammates on the other bench. *They must be wondering what's happened to me,* she realized. She was wondering the same thing herself.

The final score was a humiliating 13–3, with the only other Diamondback run accounted for by another monster shot by Allie Warheit. The sixth-grader finished with two home runs and a double. The other Diamondbacks had amassed all of one hit between them, and that one was a dribbler by Dorien Day.

After the game, Coach Beigelman gathered his battered troops for a pep talk. "We'll get 'em next time," he assured the downcast girls. "You all looked good out there. We just lost to a powerhouse team, that's all."

Kelly doubted it. Sure, the Devil Rays were awesome. With Laurie Solomon throwing like a windmill whirlwind, none of the other teams in the league were likely to do much better against them.

But the way the Diamondbacks had played, they weren't likely to be a winning team, in this league or any other.

Kelly trudged off the field, studiously avoiding her friends on the Devil Rays. She saw her mom's station wagon parked on the street and made her way quickly toward it.

"Hey! Kelly!" She turned around to see Allie trotting toward her. Kelly turned away again, but Allie kept coming.

"Nice game," Kelly managed to tell her.

"Thanks!" Allie said, flashing a brilliant smile. "Um, you too. . . ." Her voice faded, as she realized the hollowness of what she was saying.

"Yeah, right," Kelly said. "I stunk. Worse than anybody."

"Come on, anyone can have a bad game," Allie said consolingly. "It must have been nerve-racking for you, facing your old team. I'd have played tight, too, if it was me."

Kelly looked up at her and managed a faint smile. "Thanks," she said. "That's nice of you to say."

"You'll be your old self next game, you'll see," Allie assured her.

"Yeah. Well, you keep up whatever you're doing,

okay?" Kelly told her. "You played awesome." Clapping Allie on the arm, Kelly hoisted her bat and glove over her shoulder and made for her mom's car.

Ugh. She could see already that Ken was there, too, sitting in the front passenger seat. Why did he have to be there now, of all times? Wasn't it bad enough that she was a total flop, and embarrassed in front of all her old friends? Why did her mom have to bring her dorky new boyfriend to witness her humiliation?

Kelly opened the rear door, threw her stuff inside, and climbed in.

"Hi there!" her mom said chirpily. "How'd it go?"

"Crummy," Kelly said. "I don't want to talk about it."

"That bad, huh?" her mom said pityingly. "Sorry, honey. It'll get better next time."

"Can't get much worse," Kelly agreed, sinking into the seat.

But she was wrong. Later that afternoon, her mom called her into the kitchen. "Listen, Kelly," she said. "You know spring break is in ten days, and Ken and I were thinking — well, you've probably noticed that we've been getting pretty close. . . ."

Kelly rolled her eyes and sighed heavily to show how she felt about *that*.

Her mom ignored her reaction. "And we thought we'd like to go away together and spend some quality time in a nice, quiet resort —"

"Forget it," Kelly quickly told her. "I'm not going anywhere with *him.*"

"Well, that's just it," her mom went on. "We knew you probably wouldn't want to go, so —"

"Who said I didn't want to go?" Kelly countered.

"But you just said —"

"I said I didn't want to go with *him!*"

"Nora?" Ken's voice came from upstairs. "Everything okay down there?"

"Fine, darling," her mom called back. "Kelly and I are just discussing our plans for spring break."

"Oh, good!" came the reply.

Kelly stared intently at her mom, waiting for what was to come next. "So you're going away to Shangri-la with lover boy," she said sarcastically. "And what am I supposed to do? Stay home by myself?"

"Well, that's just it," her mom said, trying to put a hand on Kelly's shoulder. Kelly moved back, shaking off the hand. "We thought," said her mom, "that maybe you'd like to spend the week at a softball camp, seeing how much you love the game and all. . . ."

"Softball camp? Are you nuts? I already know how to play softball!" Kelly felt like throwing something, but there was nothing handy except for kitchen knives. So she banged her fist on the fridge instead. Fridge magnets flew in all directions.

"Kelly, honey —" her mom began.

"I'm not going to any stupid camp!" Kelly screamed at the top of her lungs. "And you can't make me! Forget it!"

She could hear Ken clomping down the stairs. "What is going on down here?" he yelled as he came storming into the kitchen. "Nora, are you okay?"

"I'm fine, sweetheart," her mom told him. "Kelly's not happy about our plans, that's all."

"I'm not going to any stupid softball camp!" Kelly repeated for his benefit.

"You'll go wherever your mother and I decide," Ken was quick to reply. "Whether you like it or not."

"You don't tell me what to do!" Kelly shouted in his face. "You're not my father, okay? I don't have to listen to you!"

"Ken . . . ," her mom started to interrupt.

"I can handle this!" Ken insisted. "Obviously, she

hasn't got enough respect to listen to her mother. But I'm not going to let her treat you like that!"

"You can't stop me, you jerk!" Kelly shrieked. He reached out to put a restraining hand on her arm, but she yanked it away. "Don't you touch me! I wish you'd never met Mom. You're a stupid twerp, and I hate you!" Turning to her mother, she added, "I hate both of you! And I'm not going anywhere! I'd rather die!"

Now she'd gone and done it. She'd told Ken exactly what she thought of him, and there was no taking it back. She stormed up to her room and slammed the door behind her. Then she collapsed on her bed and let all the bitter heartache pour out of her.

She was a loser, a total loser. She couldn't hit anymore — her main claim to fame was gone. She was on a team full of fellow losers, and her mom had a loser for a boyfriend. And now she was going to have to go to a camp full of losers for a week, while her mom and lover boy smooched on some secluded beach!

Well, forget it! She wasn't sure how she could stop it, but somehow she was going to break up their relationship. At this point, what did she have to lose?

8

The next two days were agony for Kelly. At school, she avoided her old friends, who didn't exactly go out of their way to seek her out. Kelly guessed they were as embarrassed about her performance as she was.

At home, things were even worse. Her mom and Ken, instead of talking to her, left her a note, jointly signed, telling her that she was going to camp for spring break, whether she wanted to or not. After Kelly thrashed around for a way out of her dilemma, she finally broke down and called Sue Jeffers to ask if she could spend the break with her family.

"Um, sorry, Kel, but we're going to Florida," Sue informed her.

"I could come with you!" Kelly suggested boldly.

"Hmm. Would your mom pay for your fare and stuff?" Sue asked.

That stopped Kelly. Maybe her mom would have paid, if Kelly hadn't blown up at her and Ken the other night. But as things stood, Kelly couldn't imagine her mom being so generous. "I could ask," she told Sue. But she never did. When she saw her mom next, Kelly couldn't get up the nerve.

Kelly realized by now that she would have to go along with the plan and get shipped off to this loser camp, wherever it was. Only one thought consoled her. However bad it was, being with her mom and Ken would be even worse.

As for the Diamondbacks, their second game was on Thursday afternoon, against last year's champs, the Giants. Kelly was dreading the encounter, but she needn't have been so down about it.

As it turned out, the Giants were a pale shadow of their former selves. The majority of their great players had gone on to the eighth-grade league, and the team was now made up mostly of sixth-graders. They had one pitcher who threw windmill-style, but the girl was so wild that she kept walking player after player. By the time the Giants' coach signaled for a relief pitcher, she had walked in three runs — and it was still only the first inning!

The Giants scored four runs in the first off

Dorothy Barad. Dorothy couldn't seem to master the art of windmill pitching, but stubbornly refused to throw slow-pitch. In the top of the second, the Diamondbacks loaded the bases with two walks and a lined single by Allie Warheit off the Giants' slow-pitch reliever.

Kelly came up to the plate, spat on her hands, and hoisted the bat over her shoulder. This was her meat and potatoes — slow-pitch batting-practice pitches, right over the plate. She turned on the first one, letting out all the anger she'd built up over the past two days, and smacked it way, way over the left fielder's head!

The crowd let out a whoop, and Kelly ran for all she was worth. As she rounded third, she saw Allie at the plate, yelling, "Slide! Slide!" Kelly slid, and the throw came seconds too late. She'd walloped a grand-slam home run!

The Diamondbacks kept on scoring. In the fourth inning, Kelly hit another home run. This time it was a solo shot, because Allie had cleared the bases ahead of her with a two-run blast. Unfortunately, the Giants kept scoring off Dorothy Barad and Marie del Toro, who came on to replace her in the third.

The final score was a hair-raising 13–12, but the D'backs had held on to notch their first victory. Kelly had six RBIs and Allie had two — but the main thing was, Kelly had come back from her miserable first-game performance. Sooner or later, word would get back to her old pals on the Devil Rays, and her reputation would be somewhat restored.

It was a huge relief, and Kelly couldn't help feeling generous. When Allie came over to congratulate her afterward, Kelly gave her a big hug and invited her to Sammy's for an ice-cream sundae.

"You mean it? Wow — sure!" Allie said, flashing that brilliant smile of hers. At the moment, Kelly didn't care that she was a sixth-grader. Allie was an awesome player, and Kelly was mighty glad there was someone else on her team who could really play the game.

As they sat at Sammy's, wolfing down their sundaes, Kelly couldn't help noticing that Allie didn't look like a sixth-grader. She could easily have passed for an eighth-grader, in fact. Kelly didn't even flinch when Karen Haynes came in and saw the two of them together. So what if she had a sixth-grader for a friend? Who cared?

They talked about softball and school and finally, inevitably, about guys. Actually, it was Allie who brought it up, asking if there was anybody Kelly especially liked.

There wasn't, really. Kelly had gone out with a few guys over the past year, but she hadn't had a good crush in months. Not since Larry Budnick, and he'd turned out to be a real dud, too.

"So, what about you?" she asked Allie. And when the other girl flashed a small, sly grin, Kelly knew there was somebody Allie had set her sights on. Probably some skinny little sixth-grade kid, Kelly thought, amused.

"Well, there is this guy. He goes to school with us, but he's older than me. . . ."

"How much older?" Kelly asked.

"Um . . . he's in eighth grade. . . ."

"Really?"

"Promise you won't tell anybody? It's so embarrassing. If he knew I liked him, it would be all over the school, and I'd have to dig myself a hole and jump into it."

"I won't tell," Kelly promised, really curious now. It amused her no end that Allie had a crush on an eighth-grader. That was so cute! "So, who is he?"

"He's this kid, Ryan Randall," Allie confessed, blushing almost purple. "Do you know him?"

Did she *know* him? Did she ever! Kelly almost spat out her ice cream, she was so stunned. She coughed, pretending to have swallowed down the wrong pipe.

"Are you okay?" Allie asked, concerned.

"Um, yeah," Kelly lied. She could feel a cold sweat breaking out on her forehead.

"So, do you know him?" Allie asked again.

"Um . . . no, not really," Kelly lied. "I mean, I've seen him around. I know who he is."

"Isn't he a dream?" Allie said, sighing and narrowing her big, brown eyes.

"Well . . . I guess he's kind of cute," Kelly admitted. He was more than cute, and she knew it, but she wasn't going to give Allie the satisfaction of saying so.

"Of course, I've got no chance of even meeting him. But I was thinking maybe I'd go to one of his baseball games and kind of, I don't know, bump into him or something. Or do you think that's too, like, forward?" Allie asked.

"I don't know, do what you want. But, I mean . . ."

"Never mind. It was just a thought, that's all. Forget I said anything."

"Okay, then," Kelly said, happy to drop the subject. She pushed her sundae away. Suddenly, she'd lost her appetite entirely. She wasn't sure exactly why, but she knew it had something to do with Ryan Randall.

Kelly's dad was supposed to take her to the city that weekend, to stay at his apartment and do lots of cool stuff like see shows and maybe go to a ball game at the stadium. But like he'd done so many times in the past, he failed to meet her at the appointed hour.

Kelly was willing to wait around for him, figuring he'd show up eventually. But her mom wasn't having any of it.

"Ken and I are going to the museum," she informed Kelly, "and I'm not going to leave you here alone all day."

"It won't be all day," Kelly assured her. "Dad'll come for me eventually."

Her mom scowled darkly. "That's what you say, but I've known him too long to put any trust in his promises. And you should know better, too."

She picked up the phone and dialed his number.

She stood and listened for a moment, then hung up. "His machine isn't even on. Look, Kelly, that's it. You'll have to come with us."

"But —"

"I'll take the cell phone along, and we can try him once we're in the city."

"Mom, I hate museums!"

"I'm sorry, but you'll just have to come with us. If you don't like it, you can blame your father. It's not my fault he's so irresponsible."

Kelly kicked at the air, but even she could see there was no way out of it. She was just resigning herself to a boring, awful day when they pulled up in front of Ken's house to pick him up. Ken was standing outside, and beside him stood Ryan.

"Is Ryan coming, too?" Kelly asked her mom.

"Yes, didn't I tell you? It's Ken's day to be with him. So you see? You'll have some company. It won't be so bad."

Kelly clucked her tongue, to show her mother that it didn't make any difference. But of course it did. What was going to be merely boring was now going to be tense and awkward. The last time she'd been around Ryan, she'd made a fool of herself, blushing and getting tongue-tied. She was sure he thought she was a total geek.

"Hi!" Ryan said cheerfully as he slid into the backseat next to her.

"Oh. Hi," Kelly mumbled, not daring to look at him. They sat in silence while Ken and her mom yakked it up in the front seat all the way to town.

Inside the museum, they followed the grown-ups at a safe distance. Ken was obviously a big art freak. He stood in front of each painting, going on and on about how great it was. Kelly's mom nodded, a blissful smile on her face, and occasionally said something in agreement.

"I hate museums," Ryan suddenly said to Kelly. "You?"

"Big-time," Kelly agreed, a small smile emerging at one corner of her mouth. "I'd rather be in a dentist's chair."

"The only one I like is the Natural History Museum," he told her.

"Me, too," she said, nodding. "I like those rocks that look like jewels and the stuffed dodo birds and things."

"Dino bones?" he asked, smiling broadly.

"Scary, but yeah."

"I keep thinking it would be really cool to have had one for a pet," Ryan said.

"Yeah, right?" she said with a laugh.

"Hey," he said, his voice hushed. "You wanna ditch this place and go outside? We could hang out at the fountain and wait for them."

Kelly regarded her mom and Ken, who seemed to have forgotten their children were even there. "I don't know," she said. "They might get mad."

"We could ask them," Ryan suggested. "I brought something along. . . ." He pulled a tennis ball out of his pocket. "We could, you know, toss it around."

"Cool!" Kelly said, thrilled to have a way out of this horrible boredom. "But *you* ask, okay?"

"Sure," he said, bouncing the ball once before putting it back in his pocket. "Wait here."

Soon they were outside in the sunshine, playing catch in the open air, showing off by making leaping catches and stuff while their parents strolled the cavernous halls of the museum.

Kelly was actually having fun. She darted among the people on the sidewalk, fielding pop-ups and grounders, dodging them to make quick throws back to Ryan. It was a good time she'd never expected to have, and those can be the best kind of all.

"Hey, you're not bad!" he told her when they finally sat down at one of the outdoor café tables to take a break.

"You're not so bad yourself," she complimented him back. She knew he was offhandedly telling her she was a great fielder, because she really was. And so was he. They shared a way of saying so that all real ballplayers understand.

"Want a soda?" he asked her. "My treat."

"In that case," she said as she grinned back at him, all her shyness gone after their shared good time, "I'll have an extra-super-sized one."

"You got it." He laughed, eyeing her with such genuine affection that it suddenly made her self-conscious. She started blushing and had to look down at her sneakers so he wouldn't notice.

Ryan was a really cool kid, she'd decided. She wondered how he could have a jerk like Ken for a dad, but of course she couldn't ask him that. "Um . . . how come your mom and dad got divorced?" she managed to say as they walked toward the concession stand.

Ryan's smile faded. "I, um . . . I don't really wanna talk about it. Sorry."

"Oh. Sorry I asked."

"No, it's okay. It's just — I don't know. Let's talk about something else."

"Like what?"

"Like . . . I don't know. How's your softball team?"

"We stink," Kelly said forthrightly.

"Really?"

"Well, we're one and one, but I don't think we're a .500 team, if you get my drift."

"Uh-huh."

"How about the Colts?" she asked.

"Don't you follow our games?"

"Not too closely. What are you, four and three so far?"

"Three and four," he told her. "But we're two and oh when I pitch."

"So how come they don't pitch you every game?"

"I dunno. I guess they want to give everybody a chance."

"Huh."

"You should come see me pitch sometime."

Was he asking her out? Kelly felt her cheeks burning. No, of course he wasn't. It was just a friendly gesture. He was asking her to come to one of his ball games, that was all. It wasn't a dance or something, or a movie. A guy like Ryan would never ask a seventh-grader out. Especially not one whose mom was dating his dad!

"When are you pitching next?"

"Not for a few days," he said. "I'll let you know. How about you?"

"Huh?"

"When's your team playing next?"

"Um, tomorrow. Why?"

"Well, I could come see you play."

"For real?" She felt pleased and scared at the same time. Pleased that he wanted to see more of her, and scared that she'd mess up in front of him.

But wait — why was she so worried? She'd hit two home runs in her last game, hadn't she? Allie had said Kelly was just tight playing her old team, and she'd been right, of course. What did Kelly have to be afraid of?

"So, can I come?" he asked her.

Kelly shrugged. "Sure, I guess so. It's a free country."

"I won't if you don't want me to." He looked into her eyes as if he could see right through her, and Kelly felt herself go dizzy for a moment.

She sipped hard on her soda. "No, it's okay," she finally said. "But if we lose, don't say I didn't tell you so."

"I'm coming to see *you* play, not the team," he told her, giving her a smile that shot warm lightning through her.

She smiled back, then turned away before he could see her go red in the face. "Where are those two, anyway?" she said, feigning impatience. "Isn't it gross the way they're all ooey-gooey?"

But inside, she was thinking, *He likes me!*

9

The Phillies had been last season's doormat team, the one everyone else walked all over. But no longer. This year, they had a windmill pitcher who made Laurie Solomon's fireballs look like batting-practice meatballs. If Dorien Day hadn't been hit in the leg, and Kyla Sutton in the arm, there wouldn't have been two runners on in the first for Allie Warheit to drive in with a monstrous three-run homer.

Needless to say, the D'backs fans were screaming with excitement by the time Kelly came up to bat. A 3–0 lead, and the Phillies hadn't even recorded an out yet. Their coach was already out on the mound, calming down his pitcher, while Kelly stood at the plate, taking practice swings and getting more and more nervous.

Partly, her nerves came from watching the speed

of the pitches. But mostly, it was because Ryan Randall was in the stands, sitting next to his dad and her mom, watching her. Of course, Ryan had heard what an all-star she was. Even if her mom hadn't bragged on her, it wouldn't have mattered. Everyone knew about Kelly Conroy, the female phenom, from last fall. Even the boys in school kidded her about it.

And now, Allie had gone and stolen her thunder again! Kelly knew that unless she hit a home run right there and then, she was going to look bad by comparison. She stepped into the batter's box determined to smack a four-bagger, even if there wasn't anyone on base for her to drive in.

"Stee-rike one!" yelled the umpire, after Kelly whiffed at the first pitch, a heater way over her head. A murmur went up from the fans and her teammates as they watched her flail fruitlessly at the empty air. "Stee-rike two!" came the call as the second pitch hit the catcher's mitt before she'd even gotten around on it.

Kelly braced herself. There was no way she was going to let this third pitch get by her!

Wumhph!! She heard the buzzing sound of the

ball coming her way, but she never saw the pitch that struck her out. She swung because she didn't want to go down with the bat on her shoulder, but there was no way she could ever have hit it. She was way too tense and wound up. "Stee-rike three. Yer out!" the umpire called.

Kelly trudged back to the bench, her cheeks on fire, not daring to look up in the direction of the stands. Why had she let Ryan come see her play? Last week's home runs had been an aberration — they came off a non-windmill pitcher! How had she let herself forget that?

The Phillies soon came back to take the lead, and it was all Kelly's fault. A grounder, a ball she normally would have scarfed up with no problem, dribbled right through her legs.

Then things got even worse. She came off the bag to field a ball that should have been the second baseman's, and the batter was safe, making it two on, nobody out. A three-run homer followed, and before the D'backs knew it, they were down, 6–3. Their fans had fallen silent, Ryan Randall among them.

Kelly whiffed two more times, stranding Allie Warheit both times at second, where she'd wound up as a result of two scorching doubles. Kelly didn't think she could feel any lower, until Coach Beigelman came up to her in the bottom of the fifth and told her he was putting in a sub for her.

"What?" Kelly gasped. "But —"

"I think you need to cool down a little, Kelly," he told her, patting her on the shoulder. "We'll get you back in there next game."

"Next game!" Kelly cried, and then she fell speechless. She'd never been subbed for in her entire life! It was the final humiliation. If Ryan hadn't been sitting there, she would have stormed off and walked home, right in the middle of the game, rather than sit on the bench with everyone looking at her. But with him there, she had no choice but to act like a team player.

When the game mercifully ended, the score was 7–4, Phillies. Kelly gathered up her stuff and got ready to accept condolences from Ryan, her mom, and Ken. This was going to be the worst moment of the whole miserable day.

Looking up, Kelly saw a sight that made her freeze in her tracks. There was Ryan, talking with Allie Warheit! Even from this distance, Kelly could see that Allie was flirting with him. She remembered now how Allie had talked about liking him.

At the time, Kelly had been amused by Allie's crush, thinking how stupid and hopeless it was. Now, with a budding crush of her own, it seemed threatening, not cute. She wanted to go over there and pull Allie away by that sleek, black hair of hers.

Ryan was smiling, obviously enjoying the attention. She heard him say, "You were awesome!" to Allie, obviously impressed by her performance. What would he say to Kelly? "Good game"? No possible way, unless he was the world's biggest liar.

"Hi, baby." Kelly heard her mom's voice behind her. She turned to see her mom and Ken standing there with sympathetic looks on their faces. "Rough game, huh?"

"I hate this team!" Kelly said, kicking the dirt with her cleats.

"Hey, you know what?" Ken said. "If you like, I could work with you a little on that swing of yours. I think I could help you —"

Kelly cut him off before he could finish. "Stay out of this!" she yelled at him. "Stay out of my life, okay? Just leave me alone!"

She ran off toward home, leaving her mom and

Ken standing there, and she didn't stop until the front door had slammed closed behind her.

Under the circumstances, it was almost a relief when spring break finally came and Kelly was shipped off to softball camp. All the way there on the bus, she avoided talking with any of the other kids, none of whom she knew — or wanted to know.

She was determined not to make any friends there, or even talk to anybody. But that resolve soon broke down. The counselors had them on the field all day long, except for meals, and Kelly soon found herself wrapped up in games and clinics.

Her first order of business was fixing her messed-up swing. The coaches made her open her stance, so she could get a better look at the ball. But when that only made things worse, they told her to center her feet again.

By the third day, Kelly's swing was such a mess that she was ready to give up and go home — except that no one was home to meet her. Her mom and Ken had gone off to their little romantic hideaway, and Kelly was stuck here in this torture chamber, humiliating herself day after day, unable to find her lost home-run swing.

On the fourth day, as she sat miserably on the bench alongside a bunch of chattering girls, one of the coaches came up to them and said, "Okay, girls, today we're going to teach you all how to windmill pitch."

Kelly blinked and looked up at him. It suddenly hit her. If she couldn't hit, at least she could learn how to pitch. It might give her a way out of her dilemma. She got up and followed the other girls to the mound, where one after the other, they learned the mechanics of windmill pitching.

"Okay, you stand like this," the coach instructed them, "with the heel of your front foot on the front of the rubber, and the toe of your back foot on the back of the rubber. Got that? Good."

He checked around to see that they all had it right before continuing. "Now this is key. You're only allowed to bring your hands together once during the windup, otherwise it's a 'fault.' That's like a balk. It means the base runners advance one base, or, if there aren't any runners, the pitch is called a ball.

"Okay. So, hands at your sides. Then lean back — don't move your feet, though, that's a fault too — now bring your hands up and together . . . good . . .

now the glove hand slaps the thigh on the way down, as you bring the hand with the ball back, then forward, and all the way around in a windmill motion. As you do it, the glove hand goes back from the thigh, then forward, pointing to the plate, to give you more speed and control. Follow through with the elbow of your throwing arm pointing straight out, and end with that hand on your shoulder."

One after the other, the girls all tried to mimic the complicated windup. When it came to Kelly's turn, she went into the motion, trying to visualize it as she'd seen the coach do it. Her arm wound up and back and around, and she let the ball fly. It sailed high over the backstop, at least twenty feet in the air.

"Good! Good!" the coach encouraged her, not letting Kelly sag into depression. "Just release it sooner, Kelly, when your arm is pointing at the catcher's mitt. Then, as you finish the motion, your hand should be on your shoulder. Right. Now set your feet in fielding position. That's it."

Kelly tried it again, and this time the ball whizzed from her hand with that familiar buzzing sound she'd come to fear as a hitter. The ball popped into the catcher's mitt with a loud smack. "OW!" the girl who was catching shouted. "Hey, take it easy, will you?"

"Hey, there you go!" the coach congratulated her. "Now work on that for the rest of the week, and I guarantee you, you'll have it down!"

10

Kelly spent the next three days doing nothing but pitching. She'd given up on hitting altogether. What did it matter if she struck out every time at bat? If she could pitch windmill with the best of them, the other team wouldn't be able to get a runner on base!

She arrived home and was picked up by her very tanned, happy-looking mom. When she asked Kelly how her week had been, Kelly said, "Fabulous," in her most sarcastic tone. But really, it hadn't been so bad. Not nearly as awful as she'd anticipated.

The following afternoon, right after school, was the Diamondbacks' next game. Actually, the team had played two games over the break — without Kelly — and, much to her annoyance and surprise, had won them both. "Allie's been awesome!" Dorien Day enthused. "Five homers and seven extra-base hits! Coach says he's sending her to the all-star game!"

"Fabulous," said Kelly, in the same sarcastic tone she'd used on her mom.

She hated Allie Warheit. Not only had the girl stolen her spotlight as the star of the team, but she'd had the nerve to move in on Ryan Randall, a guy who was two years older than her, two grades ahead of her — and the very same guy Kelly had developed a crush on. Worst of all, she'd shown Kelly up in front of him at the last game before vacation. Well, today Kelly was going to get some of her own back.

"Coach," she said, going up to him before the game began, "can I pitch today?"

"You?" he said, surprised. "I thought you liked playing first base."

"I do, but I went to softball camp during break and learned to pitch windmill."

"Really?" The coach grew thoughtful. "Tell you what. I don't want to hurt Marie's feelings. I promised her she could pitch today. But if she runs into any trouble, I'll put you in there in relief, okay?"

Kelly sighed in frustration, but she didn't argue with him. She felt pretty sure that Marie would run into trouble soon enough. She always did.

The D'backs' opponents were the Dodgers, a

team with a 4–1 record going into the game, their only loss being to the undefeated Devil Rays. By the third inning, they were ahead, 3–2, and had loaded the bases against Marie del Toro with nobody out. Coach Beigelman walked slowly to the mound and signaled to the ump that he was making a pitching change. Then he beckoned to Kelly.

"You sure you're ready for this?" he asked her, handing her the ball.

"Ready as I'll ever be," she answered, blowing out a deep breath.

He patted her on the back and headed for the dugout. Kelly pounded the ball into her mitt a few times, then stared in at Sarah Harden, the catcher.

"Okay, here goes," she muttered under her breath as she went into her windup.

The ball flew out of her hand and buzzed the chin of the batter, who wheeled out of its way. Sarah was so surprised that she never got her glove up. But fortunately the ball hit off the backstop and bounced right back to her, so the runner on third was unable to come home.

There was a wave of murmuring from the stands, and a few audible "Whoa"s from the base runners and the fielders. Kelly took the throw from the catcher and concentrated on her release point, the way they'd taught her at camp. This time, she whizzed the ball in right over the plate.

"Stee-rike one!" called the ump.

Kelly shook out her shoulders and stayed focused. "Stee-rike two!" shouted the ump as the batter flailed helplessly at the next pitch. One more, and Kelly had recorded her first-ever strikeout — on the very first batter she'd faced!

Next up was the Dodgers' cleanup hitter. Kelly fanned her on three straight fastballs. Now the murmuring had become cheering from the Diamondbacks, and outraged heckling from the Dodgers, who were trying to rattle her.

But Kelly was not about to be rattled. She got two strikes on the next hitter, then shook off Sarah's sign and threw a windmill change-up that totally fooled the hitter.

"Stee-rike three, you're out!" yelled the ump, and Kelly leaped into the air, pounding her fist into her glove.

Her teammates mobbed her as she reached the bench, and Coach Beigelman said, "Hey, where'd you learn to pitch like that?"

Kelly just smiled happily.

"You're awesome!" Allie said. "What were you thinking, playing first base? We need you on the mound!"

"Well, you've got me from now on," Kelly told her with a grin of genuine pleasure.

By the end of the game, Kelly had recorded twelve strikeouts, and the D'backs had recorded another victory. Amazingly, some of Kelly's teammates even made good defensive plays behind her, on the few occasions when the Dodgers actually made contact. Maybe Coach Beigelman wasn't such a loser after all, Kelly thought, wondering if she'd judged him too harshly. His policy of praise and encouragement seemed to be paying off.

The only bad thing about the game was that neither her mom nor Ryan Randall had been there to see her triumph. "Figures," Kelly muttered to herself as she saw her mom's station wagon pull up to the curb to pick her up. "I have a great game, and they miss it. I mess up, and they're right there to see the whole thing."

But she couldn't be too upset. Not today. Even though she'd struck out three times, it hadn't mattered. They'd won, and she'd been the hero. Even more important, with a record of 4–2, it looked like the Diamondbacks might even have a future.

Her mom was positively glowing, and for a moment Kelly thought it was because of her good news about the game. But no, her mom had something entirely different on her mind, as it turned out. "Honey," she said, biting her lip to keep from overflowing with pleasure, "I've got some news — big news. Are you ready?"

"Um . . . what?" Kelly asked warily.

"Ken and I have been growing closer, as you probably know. . . ."

"Yeah . . . and?"

"Well, we've talked it over — and . . . well, you see, he's living in this little apartment that's way too expensive, and we thought —"

"Don't tell me he's moving in with us," Kelly said, a lump of dread rising in her throat.

"Now, don't be like that," her mom pleaded. "He's a wonderful man, and he loves me very much. And I love him."

"Well, I don't," Kelly countered. "And I don't want him living with us!"

"Kelly, honey, it's not really your decision."

"Why not?" Kelly challenged. "Don't I get a vote?"

"I'm afraid not. Not this time. You'll get used to it in time. . . ."

"I will not!"

"You'll just have to, Kelly. You're being stubborn and contrary, and this is not up to you. You are not the parent —"

"If he's moving in, I'm moving out!" Kelly shouted, banging her fist on the dashboard. "I'm going to call Dad!"

"Fine," her mother said. "Call whomever you want. But if you think your dad is going to have anything to say about this, you're wrong. And don't get the idea you're going to go live with him. Aside from the fact that he's never around, it would mean changing schools and your whole routine. No way."

The two of them fell into a simmering, angry silence. Kelly searched her brain for a solution, but she kept coming up empty. Her good mood after the game was totally gone now. The moment her mom pulled into the driveway, Kelly got out and hopped onto her bike. She didn't know where she was going, and she didn't care so long as it was away from home.

❖   ❖   ❖

"You're not gonna win this one, Kel," Sue Jeffers advised her. "I mean, I sympathize and all, but there's no way you can go live with your dad. You know that."

Kelly sniffed back the tears that wouldn't stop coming. The two friends were sitting on Sue's front stoop, and Sue had her arm around Kelly, trying in vain to comfort her.

"I hate them so much!" Kelly fumed. "Grown-ups really bite."

"I know, I know," Sue said sympathetically.

"If I have to live with them, I'm going to make them wish they'd never met each other."

"I wouldn't go there, Kelly. Bad plan."

"Why? What's so bad about making them miserable?"

"Because if they're miserable, they're only going to make you even more miserable, that's what." Sue brushed Kelly's red hair out of her eyes. "Look, I tried that tactic once with my mom, when that guy Harry moved in. The construction guy — remember him? Anyway, making them miserable turned out to be a bad idea. Harry moved out after a couple of months, and my mom blamed me for it. She's been resenting me ever since. It's gotten so bad, I've started looking out for potential boyfriends for her. Is that pathetic, or what?"

"Well . . ."

Sue gave her a smile. "Come on, Ken's probably not as bad as all that. Hey, look at the bright side. He's Ryan Randall's dad, right?"

"Yeah, so?"

"So, Ryan's pretty cute, if you ask me. I mean, you could introduce me. . . ."

"Forget it," Kelly said, but she couldn't help cracking a smile.

"Don't tell me you haven't noticed."

"What?"

"Kelly . . ."

"Okay, so he's cute. That's not what's important. What's important is that I have to put up with his stupid father night and day, forever."

"Not necessarily forever," Sue corrected her. "Besides, if it does work out with him and your mom, at least she'll be happy. Happy parents are much more generous with their kids. It's a proven scientific fact."

"Get out of here," Kelly said, giggling and giving Sue a little shove.

Sue pretended to fall over, but she was laughing,

too. "Hey, I hear you can pitch windmill," she said. "When did this happen?"

"At camp, over the break," Kelly confessed. "Don't tell anyone, though. Only the coach knows I learned that at softball camp."

"Why lie about it?" Sue asked. But when Kelly sighed and rolled her eyes, she said, "Okay, okay, I won't say anything. You want to look like a phenom, far be it from me to spoil your party. Promise me one thing, though."

"What?"

"When we play you again, you've got to forgive me if I hit one out on you."

Kelly grinned, feeling like herself again. "You won't even see the ball," she promised Sue.

"Yeah, right."

"True," Kelly insisted. "You wait and see."

"Fine," Sue said, getting up. "Look, you'd better get home."

"I guess you're right. Thanks for humoring me."

"De nada," Sue said. "And like I said, give Ken a chance. Try being friendly with him, even if you can't stand him."

"I'll try," Kelly promised. "But you'll see. Once a jerk, always a jerk."

11

Kelly rode home, determined to make an effort to be agreeable. Sue might be right, or she might be wrong. But Kelly could see that her mom was determined to have Ken move in with them, and that being a brat about it would not get her anywhere.

She didn't have to like him, after all. She only had to share space with him. And as long as he stayed out of her hair and didn't try to be her dad, she would behave herself. At least, she would try.

He was there when she got back. He and her mom were putting the finishing touches on dinner. Kelly acted like nothing had happened, and she noticed that her mom seemed relieved and didn't take her to task about her tantrum in the car. As for Ken, he acted like nothing had happened, pretending that everything was hunky-dory.

Kelly told them how good the food smelled, and

then got busy helping to set the table. The look of gratitude on her mom's face was totally pathetic, but it gave Kelly a twisted sense of being in control. But when she invited them to watch her next softball game, they acted so enthusiastic it made her soften a little — though she didn't let them see that.

The team's next game was against the Indians, a team that was much improved from last year. Like the D'backs, they had a 4–2 record, and they were loaded with promising sixth-graders. Kelly took the mound, determined to shut down their much talked-about offense.

The first three batters to face her went down swinging. Kelly strode back to the bench as if nothing had happened, as if she did this kind of thing every day of her life. She could hear her mom and Ken cheering her on, but she didn't acknowledge them. It gave her deep satisfaction to know she was on top of her game again, even if it was in a totally different way than before.

"Hey, we've got us a windmill wizard!" Coach Beigelman crowed, slapping her on the back. "Give it up for Kelly, you guys!"

Everyone slapped her five. Now it was time for the D'backs to go to work and score some runs.

Leading off, Kyla Sutton managed to work out a walk. That brought Allie Warheit to the plate. By now, the whole league obviously knew about her hitting ability, because the Indians' pitcher stayed away from the plate, walking Allie on four pitches to get to Kelly.

That made Kelly mad. So now they were intentionally walking a sixth-grader to get to her? Well, she'd show them! Kelly strode to the plate determined to drive the runners in, with a long home run if possible.

The first pitch was in the dirt, but Kelly was all geared up, and she swung over the top of it. The second pitch was over her head, but again she went after it. Kelly could feel her frustration level rising as the blood rose to her cheeks, showing the world how embarrassed she felt.

The pitcher wound up and threw her a change-up. Kelly was way out in front and hit a soft dribbler in front of the plate. The catcher picked it up and threw to third for one out. Then the third baseman flipped it to second for a double play.

Kelly was so stunned that she forgot to run out the hit. By the time she made it to first, the ball had beaten her there. Triple play!

Kelly flung her helmet to the ground in disgust. She'd single-handedly killed her team's big first-inning rally! It had to be the first triple play in league history, and she knew everyone would be talking about it for months to come.

She didn't dare look into the stands to see how her mom and Ken were reacting. And she shook off Coach Beigelman's encouraging words. Grabbing her glove and the ball, she stormed onto the mound, brimming over with anger.

For the next five innings, she tossed fireballs past every Indian hitter. Their bats never stood a chance. One after another, they went down in futility. A few even tried to bunt, but their attempts were either popped up or went foul.

When Kelly came up to bat next time, she went to the plate with an idea. If the opposing batters could try bunting, so could she. She laid a perfect one down and made it to first without a throw. Then she stole second on the next pitch, and stole third on the pitch after that. Marie del Toro's pathetic ground ball was enough to score her, and the D'backs took a 1–0 lead. Kelly slapped everyone five so hard that her own hands hurt.

She cruised through six innings that day, pitching a perfect game until the last out, when the Indians' cleanup hitter got lucky enough to hit an infield single. The next batter popped up to short. Allie Warheit put it away and leaped into the air. "Yes! A one hitter!" she screamed, and ran to hug Kelly. The entire team mobbed her, but all Kelly could think about was the stupid triple play she'd hit into.

She accepted their congratulations, though, and those of her mom and Ken as well. "You were awesome!" Ken told her.

"Thanks," she said, pounding the ball into her mitt.

"I've never seen anyone your age pitch that well! I'm gonna start telling people I taught you myself."

Kelly snorted at his feeble joke, but she was pleased at the compliment.

"You know," he went on, "like I told you before, I think I could help you with your hitting. . . ."

Kelly looked at him sharply. "No thanks," she told him.

"It wouldn't take much of an adjustment, you know," he said.

"I said, 'No thanks,'" she repeated. "What part of

115

that don't you understand?" In spite of her best efforts, she knew she was being rude to him. Somehow, he just brought out the worst in her.

"Look, I've tried to be nice to you," he said, his voice taking on a chilly tone. "But you've frustrated me at every turn. Now we're going to be living together. So if you can't find a way to be pleasant, you'd better not say anything to me at all."

"Fine!" she said, but she was already talking to his back, because he'd turned and walked away from her.

What's the use of trying to be nice to a guy like that? she asked herself. *He wouldn't appreciate it, anyway.* She could see now that there was no way they would ever get along.

"Hey, Kelly!"

Kelly turned around and saw Ryan beckoning to her from the stairway. She had just emerged from her English class and had only four minutes to get to Spanish, so she jogged quickly over to meet him.

"Hey, what's up?" she said, brushing back a stray lock of hair that had fallen over her face.

"You got a minute?" he asked.

"Um, yeah, I've got study hall next," she lied.

116

"Cool. I've, um, been wanting to talk to you. . . ."

"What about?"

"Um, well . . . you know the May dance?"

Kelly felt a sharp thrill surge inside her. "Yeah?"

"Well . . . I was thinking of asking you to go to it?"

Yes! she thought. "Uh-huh?"

"But, um, like, well, I figured, with our parents going out and all, it would be too weird for us to start dating."

No! she thought, crestfallen. "Yeah, I guess it would be kind of weird . . . ," she agreed, not really meaning a word she was saying.

"So, I, um, kind of thought I'd ask that girl Allie instead."

"Allie? Allie Warheit?"

"Um, yeah."

"She's in sixth grade, Ryan!"

"I know, but —"

"Whatever," Kelly said, shaking her head in exasperation.

"I hope you aren't too upset about it. . . ."

"Why should I be upset?" she asked, trying to keep a lid on her emotions. "I'm just, I don't know, grossed out, is all."

"Why?"

"Cuz she's in sixth grade! It's like, *eeuw!*"

"She doesn't look like a sixth-grader."

"Whatever. Like I said, it's your call. But talk about weird — *that's* weird."

"If you say so. I just thought I'd let you know. . . ."

"Why should I care? You don't need my permission."

"I know. Even so, just thought I'd give you a heads up."

"Yeah, well, thanks."

Thanks for nothing! she thought bitterly. *That stupid Allie Warheit — I could kill her for this!*

"Oh, by the way," Ryan said, stopping her as she was about to run off to Spanish class — late, thanks to him. "My dad asked me to talk to you about —"

"What, was he complaining about me?" she asked, openly hostile now.

"Well, not exactly . . . but —"

"I don't care what he thinks," she said, turning to go again.

"He's not a bad guy, my dad," Ryan said, stopping her. "He really isn't, whatever you think. I mean, he has his flaws, sure. He's a little too strict —"

"You can say that again."

"But he's got his good side, too."

"Yeah, right."

"He does, believe me. Like, for instance, he was always there for me, growing up."

"Oh, please — bring out the violins," Kelly said sarcastically.

"Okay, make fun of me," Ryan said, "but it's true. For instance, he's never, ever missed one of my ball games."

That got Kelly where she lived. She felt a pang in her gut as she thought of all the times her dad hadn't shown up for one of *her* games, even though he'd promised to be there.

"And he taught me everything I know about the game," Ryan went on. "He's the best coach ever."

"Huh," Kelly said noncommittally.

"You know, it wouldn't kill you to let him work with you on your swing. I know he asked if you wanted help."

"I don't need any help, from him or anybody else, thank you."

"Whatever." Now it was Ryan's turn to be sarcastic. "But think about it. Like I said, he's not all bad. Not even half bad, really. If you gave him a chance, you might find out I'm right."

"Yeah, well, thanks," Kelly said, not even looking at him as she walked away. "See you around sometime."

"Sorry if I upset you," he called after her.

"You didn't," she assured him. The tears were forcing their way out of her eyes, but luckily she had her back turned to him, so he couldn't see how hurt she was.

12

All day long, Ryan's words burned into Kelly's consciousness. She wondered if perhaps she'd judged Ken too harshly. After all, Ryan was his son. He'd lived with Ken for years before the breakup, and if he thought Ken was a good guy, then maybe he was.

Several things about her conversation with Ryan were eating at Kelly. Worst of all, of course, was that he was asking Allie to the May dance instead of her. That was a slap in the face, especially since he said that he'd wanted to ask Kelly in the first place, but didn't because of their parents going out.

Kelly wondered if that was true. She thought that perhaps the real reason Ryan was asking Allie instead of her was that Allie was a better ballplayer than she was. Ouch. It hurt just to think that, but Kelly couldn't escape the truth. Sure, she was as good a fielder as Allie, and she used to be as good a hitter. But she wasn't anymore. These days, she was a total loss at the plate.

Kelly thought again of what Ryan had said about his dad being a great coach. "He taught me everything I know about the game," he'd said.

Maybe she was just being stubborn. For the first time, humiliating as it would be, Kelly considered asking Ken to help her with her swing.

No, she couldn't. She just couldn't! Not after the way she'd treated him. He'd just tell her to get lost, and he'd be right, too. If anyone had talked to Kelly like that, she certainly wouldn't give her the time of day if she asked for help.

But after all, he was supposedly in love with her mom. Maybe, for the sake of family harmony, he'd be willing to forgive and forget . . . *if* she could get up the courage to ask.

That night, she got her chance. After dinner, her mom had to leave for a meeting of her women's group, a bunch of professional moms who got together every month for encouragement and dessert. Kelly had always thought of it as just an excuse for her mom to socialize. But it usually meant a night when she could watch TV all evening without her mom complaining, so it was fine with Kelly.

Tonight, though, her mom had left Ken in charge. For a moment, Kelly felt the automatic impulse to act nasty about it, but she restrained herself. It gave her a weird kind of satisfaction to see the surprised looks on their faces when she didn't act up.

A few minutes after her mom had left, while Ken was busy doing the dishes, Kelly came into the kitchen. "Need any help with those?" she asked pleasantly.

Ken gave her a startled look. "Er, thanks!" he said. "That's nice of you to offer, but I'm almost done here."

"Oh." She opened the fridge. "Want me to cut up some fruit for dessert?"

"Yeah, that'd be great." Ken stood there watching her, a dish in one hand and a towel in the other, not moving.

"Um, remember the other day, when you offered to give me some pointers on my swing?" she asked, fishing out some apples.

"Sure," he said, beginning to wipe off the dish.

"Could you — I mean, would you mind? I know my swing's kind of a mess. . . ."

He put down the dish and the towel. "Right now?" he asked.

"Well, I don't know. . . . It's kind of dark out."

"That's nothing. We can turn on the porch light. Come on."

"Cool. I've got a bat in the garage." Kelly ran to get it, while Ken dried his hands off on the towel. Moments later, they met on the porch.

"Come on down here, in the light," he told her. "Now, take a swing for me. Right, like that."

She swung hard, visualizing the ball arcing into the night sky.

"See, you've got a great natural power swing," Ken told her.

"Yeah, right. That's why I can't hit for beans."

"You hit fine, until you started seeing windmill pitching," he pointed out. "Isn't that true?"

"Well, yeah. So? I can't catch up with it, is all. So that's that."

"Not necessarily," Ken corrected her. "That's why I wanted to work with you on it. See, windmill pitching's a lot faster, so you have to cut down your swing a little."

"Uh-uh," Kelly balked. "That's what they told me at that softball camp. It messed up my swing even worse."

"Well, there's nothing wrong with the swing that I

can see," Ken insisted. "Let me see how it looks when you cut it down."

She showed him. "Aha!" he said. "See, you're not shifting your weight when you take the shorter swing. You've still got to make the shift if you want to hit with any power."

"How can I do that?"

"Well, you've got to start it earlier, and cut out the hitch."

"Hitch?"

"Yeah, you know how you drop the bat a little when you start the swing? It's kind of a timing mechanism for you — but if you lift your front foot instead, you'll still be able to time the swing without making it take longer."

She tried it a few times, and he made small adjustments until he was satisfied she had it down. "There," he said. "Now, the other thing is, you're not picking up the pitcher's release point."

"Huh?"

"You're following all that motion, and you're not seeing the ball as it leaves the pitcher's hand. You've got to stare at the point where you know the release will be, and ignore all the motion around it."

"Okay . . . ," she said doubtfully.

"Look, when's your next game?"

"I don't know. I'll have to check."

They went inside, and she consulted her schedule. "Oh, great," she moaned. "We're playing the Devil Rays again. Day after tomorrow."

"Well, that gives us a day, at least. Can you come with me to the ball field after school?"

"The other teams'll be playing there."

"Okay, how about someplace else?"

"Um, I guess the school yard would be okay."

"Fine. I'll meet you there after school with your bat and a bag of balls. I can throw you some windmill pitches, so you can get used to the idea."

"Cool!"

Her enthusiastic response came as a complete surprise to her — and to him, too, she could see by the look on his face. Maybe Ryan was right about him and maybe her mom wasn't so stupid after all. Maybe Kelly had made up her mind too soon about Ken.

She went to bed that night full of confusing thoughts and didn't sleep much at all. When she did, she had nightmares about the upcoming game against the Devil Rays.

✿   ✿   ✿

By the end of their practice session the following day, Kelly had begun to get her old confidence back. She was walloping pitch after pitch, sending balls rocketing off the wall of the school, way at the other end of the school yard. If she hit anything like this against the Devil Rays, she was going to surprise a lot of people.

And though it took something to admit it, she was having a good time with Ken. It was weird, she thought in one of her more contemplative moments. She would never have believed he could be this much fun.

Maybe he'd been as uncomfortable around her as she'd been around him. It couldn't have been easy for him, she reflected, coming into their house and trying to act like a part of their family, especially when Kelly had made his every move that much more difficult. She felt sorry now that she'd been so mean to him, especially since he was being so nice to her.

When the time for the Devil Rays game rolled around, Ken and her mom were both there in the stands, cheering her on. Kelly sort of wished they weren't there, since it was really distracting knowing she had to perform or they would see her fall flat on her face again.

On the other hand, the tips she'd gotten from Ken in the past two days had made her feel much calmer about her skills. She felt sure she could at least make contact with Laurie's pitches.

And on the other side, the Devil Rays were in for a surprise when she stepped onto the mound. "Windmill Wizard," Coach Beigelman had called her. Well, today she was going to show her old team some of her new magic.

There they all were — Sue Jeffers, Karen Haynes, Laurie Solomon, Beth Parks, Nina Montone — all her old friends and teammates in their blue-and-green uniforms. And here she was, in her yellow-and-black Diamondbacks jersey, ready to do battle with them.

The D'backs were the visiting team, so they batted first. Laurie hit the mound and started to warm up, her windmill pitches popping in the mitt of Danielle Lauritsen, the Rays' catcher. "Attababy!" Danielle shouted encouragingly, even as she shook the pain out of her glove hand.

Dorien Day walked slowly to the plate. As she did,

Coach Beigelman yelled, "Let's go, D'backs! Let's show 'em what we're made of!"

They were made of pretty good stuff, Kelly had come to see. A 5–2 record going in, while it wasn't a perfect 7–0 like the Devil Rays', was not exactly chopped liver, either.

Dorien had never been a great hitter for them, but she somehow usually found a way to get on base. Today was no different. After taking two called strikes, Dorien kept fouling off pitch after pitch. Finally, on the tenth pitch of the at bat, she worked out a walk.

Kyla Sutton was not so patient, nor so good a contact hitter. She struck out on three pitches. Allie Warheit was up next. "Come on, Allie!" Kelly found herself yelling. As much as the sixth-grade phenom irritated her, they were teammates now, and this was war.

But Laurie Solomon had no intention of letting Allie beat the Rays. She pitched carefully to her — so carefully that Allie walked on four pitches.

Oh, so that's how it is, Kelly thought bitterly. *They'd rather pitch to pathetic old me, huh? Well, fine. Bring it on, Laurie.* She strode angrily to the plate, going over in her head all the things Ken had taught her.

She paid no attention as Laurie went into her herky-jerky windup. Instead she focused only on the spot where the ball would be released. At the same time, she raised her front foot, timing her swing. The ball whizzed toward her, looking to Kelly more like a basketball than the pea it had resembled of late. She swung hard, then heard the sweet ping of aluminum smashing cowhide.

A roar went up from the crowd as the ball soared skyward. "Look at that!" Kelly heard Coach Beigelman raving. "Wow!"

Kelly ran toward first base, but she might as well have walked. The ball was way gone, and it wasn't coming back. Kelly reached home plate and was mobbed by her jubilant teammates well before the left fielder had retrieved the ball from beyond field number three.

"Whoo-hooo!" Allie Warheit roared, double high fiving Kelly. "Oh, baby! What a shot!"

The Conroy Comet, her old teammates used to call those moon shots of hers. Well, it had been a long time since she'd hit one, and never off windmill pitching. Kelly looked up into the stands and found Ken, standing with her mom and applauding. She gave him a smile and the thumbs-up sign before heading back to the dugout.

Laurie soon settled down and retired the side. Now it was time for Kelly to do a little windmilling of her own. She headed to the mound, full of confidence and enthusiasm. Suddenly, she wanted more than anything to beat her old team, to ruin their perfect record. It hit her that until today, she'd still seen herself as part of the Devil Rays.

Now, for the first time all season, she felt herself a true Diamondback. She wasn't on the wrong team after all, any more than she was in the wrong family.

She mowed down the Devil Rays in the first, and again in the second and third. Three innings, nine strikeouts. A large crowd gathered around field number four, where they were playing. They had heard what was going on and came to witness her performance.

In the fourth inning, Kelly came to bat again. Ahead of her, Allie had just hit a home run to make the score 4–0. This time, Kelly did not go after the first pitch, knowing that Laurie wasn't about to give her anything fat to hit. Instead, she let the count go to 3–1 before smacking a sharp double to center field.

She didn't score that inning, but in the sixth, when she came up for the third time, she drove in Allie, who had doubled ahead of her, with another Conroy Comet. The score was now 6–0, D'backs, and an upset was in the making.

The Devil Rays finally broke up her no-hitter in the seventh and last inning, with two infield dribblers that went for singles. Then Kelly struck out Sue Jeffers for her twelfth K, to end the game with a shutout. Kelly leaped into the air, throwing her mitt skyward as she danced on the mound with Allie and her other D'back teammates.

The stunned Devil Rays hung their heads, unable to believe they'd just been obliterated. It was their first loss of the season, and their aura of invincibility would never be the same.

Who knew how the season would work out? Kelly didn't, but she didn't even care. The important thing was, she was a Diamondback now. Ken, her mom's new boyfriend, had helped her get there, by making her a whole player again, someone who could hit as well as pitch and play defense.

So what if he wasn't perfect? At least he wasn't a

total idiot, like she'd thought he was. If her mom liked him, Kelly would accept him, even if he was a semi-jerk some of the time. After all, she wasn't exactly perfect herself. She'd welcome him into their home, especially if he kept on coaching her to be a better ballplayer.

"Hey, Kelly!"

Kelly turned around and saw Ryan standing there, smiling broadly at her.

"Hi!" she said, feeling her cheeks flush red. "Were you watching the game?"

"Uh-huh! I caught those home runs of yours. You were awesome!"

"Um, thanks," she said, kicking a little dirt up with her cleats. "Your dad really helped."

"He did?" Ryan asked, sounding genuinely surprised.

"Yeah. Didn't he tell you?"

"Uh-uh. I guess he didn't want anyone to know."

"Oh. Well, that was nice of him, huh?"

"I told you he wasn't a bad guy."

"Yeah, well, I guess you were right," Kelly admitted. Then she saw Allie smiling and waving to Ryan, who waved back. "So, did you ask Allie to the May dance?" she asked.

"Um, no. I kind of changed my mind about that," he said. "I thought I'd just show up solo and dance with whoever."

"Oh," Kelly said, secretly pleased. She had been planning to do the same thing.

"So, um, I was wondering, maybe you and I could, like, go to a movie or something sometime . . . ," he said. Looking up, Kelly saw that his cheeks had a bit of red in them, too.

"I thought you said . . . ," she began.

"I know," he said. "But, well, we could go to a movie over in Canterville. Nobody knows us there."

"Cool!" Kelly said, allowing herself a secret smile. "Hey, I can keep a secret if you can!"

"Excellent!" Ryan said. "Well, see you around, then."

"Right. Bye." She waved as he wandered off, feeling a rush of happiness wash over her.

"He's so cute, isn't he?" Allie's voice came from over her shoulder.

"Oh, he's okay, I guess," Kelly answered offhandedly.

"Come on, D'backs," Coach Beigelman said, smiling broadly. "Let's line up and shake hands!"

They lined up, a winning team, to shake the hands

of the team they'd beaten. Kelly stuck her hand out to slap her old buddies five. When she got to Sue Jeffers, she stopped to give her a hug. "Hey," she said, "don't worry, you guys are still the team to beat."

"Yeah," Sue said glumly. "Well, you were awesome, girl."

"Thanks."

"See you in the playoffs, huh?"

"Yeah. See you there."

Kelly walked toward her mom and Ken, feeling like she was on top of the world. What had she been so worried about, anyway? Life was change, and nothing ever stood still forever. She had a new team and a new member of the family — and maybe even a new secret boyfriend.

Life was good, and as long as she stayed loose and went with the flow, it was only going to get better.